Space Apples

Space Apples

SPACE, STORY AND A COLLECTION
OF SPIRITED WORD SALAD

Christopher J. Martindale

PALMETTO
PUBLISHING
Charleston, SC
www.PalmettoPublishing.com

Copyright © 2024 by Christopher J Martindale

All rights reserved

No portion of this book may be reproduced, stored in a retrieval system, or transmitted in any form by any means–electronic, mechanical, photocopy, recording, or other–except for brief quotations in printed reviews, without prior permission of the author.

First Edition

Paperback ISBN: 9798822966079

Space Apples

A COLLECTION OF STORY AND
SPIRITED WORD SALAD

Andross A New Dawn 1

Love From Above 55

Stream of Citizen 65

Speculation of Crazy Ideas. .95

Dissent Into Madness (poetry) 127

Stream of Crazy. 235

In a distant world, in a far-off planet, there is a place for scholarship. On this same planet, there are many counteractive ideas. There are business exploits, social co-opted enterprise, scientific research and discovery. Each with competing ideas and their champions. Even on a planet as gigantic as Planet Xavier, the world can seem too small for such larger-than-life figures... Hope then, would be even further from it. On a distant, moon named Andross. In its Terraformation it might bring a new kind of meaning to life in this galaxy... If the champions can pull it off.

ANDROSS: A NEW DAWN

Chapter 1: Planet Xavier 1
Chapter 2: Meet Max, Ben's Roommate 6
Chapter 3: Meet Dexter 11
Chapter 4: Ivy's League 13
Chapter 5: Meet Landon. 17
Chapter 6: Landon Effect 20
Chapter 7: What's Brewing? .26
Chapter 8: Dexter Revisited .29
Chapter 9: Flash Forward 32
Chapter 10: What's Cookin'?. 34
Chapter 11: Tara's Way 36
Chapter 12: The Fire. 39
Chapter 13: Waterlogged. 41
Chapter 14: Ben's Bender 43
Chapter 15: Fire Brand 45
Chapter 16: Launch to Rhea .48
Chapter 17: The Stay in Rhea 50
Chapter 18: You're Breaking Up 52

ANDROSS: A NEW DAWN

Chapter 1: Planet Xavier 1
Chapter 2: Meet Max, Ben's Roommate 6
Chapter 3: Meet Dexter 11
Chapter 4: Ivy's League 13
Chapter 5: Meet Landon 17
Chapter 6: Landon Effect 20
Chapter 7: What's Brewing? 26
Chapter 8: Dexter Revisited 29
Chapter 9: Flash Forward 32
Chapter 10: What's Cookin'? 34
Chapter 11: Tara's Way 36
Chapter 12: The Fire 39
Chapter 13: Waterlogged 41
Chapter 14: Ben's Bender 43
Chapter 15: Fire Brand 45
Chapter 16: Launch to Rhea 48
Chapter 17: The Stay in Rhea 50
Chapter 18: You're Breaking Up 52

Chapter 1

PLANET XAVIER

In the cold vacuum of space, life can seem delicate and inconsequential. One human life standing against the grand chaos of galaxy's being birthed. Cascades of light in a myriad of majesties shining from gas giants. Pulsing energy flares shooting wildly on their surface, barely containing the celestial energy. One could get lost in it, if there wasn't a force as grounding as, well, gravity. Gravity on the scholarly planet of Xavier was 3 quarters of the gravity on old world Earth. Many of the young people on scholar planet Xavier had very lofty ambitions as well. On this planet, in the year 3,141, if you are of reasonable ability, life is yours. There are many technical specialties for someone to find their niche and there are an increasing number of missions in a well-funded series of public and private exploits. It is a breeding ground for corporate recruitment, as well as scholarly advancements funded by The Xavier Planetary Federation. A government founded by a corporate entity from "The New Union of Liberated States" founded in the 26th century. The government is strictly focused on defense and the welfare of its people. The space mission tax credit system is the best in the galaxy and hence sprung a plethora of exploits, becoming a sort of hub in this fashion. The missions ranged from the mundane satellite launches and asteroid mining to the lucrative exploration and search for habitable planets. With the increasing privatization of space, the search for and rehabilitation of said planets became proprietary knowledge and, in some cases, clandestine. This was the case for the terraforming of Andross, but before that, the coordinator of the mission meets a key member.

He was on a leisurely stroll through the university after his supply chain economics class, wandering absent mindedly to the nearest coffee bar. This coffee bar happened to be, "The Jitter Bean". It was a 20th century themed bar with an Earthly hand-carved piano of the 26th century. There were gauged wrought iron steel chairs bent in vine like curvature and sitting in them was a gathering of college men and women. At the front of the over-hang of the bar's sign was a banner. "Come for The Free Coffee, Stay for The Experience". in finer print underneath, it read, "If you can guess where it's bean, you get to chat with the creator! Hint: You are what you drink." Ben couldn't resist rubbing elbows with innovators especially when it came with a challenge. With the question in mind, Ben walks closer to the carafes filled with new coffee. The label read, "Buzz Brew Fermented Coffee". There was a hum of chatter at every table. He grabbed a carafe and a 16oz cup and poured it in. Curious about its creator, he scanned the room for the someone who could organize so many people around a new brew. He scanned to the left, blondes and brunettes sitting at tables drinking their coffee. He scanned to the right, and looked behind the carafes to four women discussing, gesturing, and pivoting around a center focus. A woman in black garb was there. She had black hair, a bob cut, and a pendant like emerald jewel dangling low beneath her turtleneck. She had horned rim glasses on her nose showing her naked green eyes. Pale white skin and bright red lipstick drew his eyes for a moment. Her look was to her left. Her jeans were black too, skintight, all the way to her leathery shoes. He was feeling for her hook, everyone had one and hers was coming to him. She had a small silver watch but no bangles, showing pragmatism and a reserved taste. She was gorgeous, with the slightest hunch. She must either be typing at a desk often, reading a book, or both.

This wasn't very revelatory for a university. She was likely a student, and that alone would do well for conversation. Maybe an alternatively ultra-casual type with a passionate mind for projects would do the trick. Ben was wearing jeans and a suit jacket, but he had a plaid jacket with elbow patches from a confidant, in his briefcase. She notices his stare and readjusts a little behind the coffee grinder, blocking his gaze. Ben, takes a gulp of his coffee, unzips his briefcase, throws on the tweed jacket and walks over to a map next to a bookcase. He looks over the countries, on it, under the banner. He takes this very seriously. He glosses over the countries with a tenuous grasp for Earth countries. He takes his first sip and is beguiled. He takes another sip, and another, and another. His glossing shifts to poignant attention. Eyes darting between countries, he picks up details in the geography he'd normally never notice. He reads the margins, and the borders of the countries start to clarify. He looks it over once more and words start to dawn on him. Something he read on a Starbird cup comes to the forefront of his mind. It was the "origins of coffee". He traced a passage from its origin in "Ethiopia", to its trade across a desert and forthwith to the coasts of "continents" where the coffee trade went on. Something to his left caught his eye, maybe a clump of dust, though he followed it to a larger single continent. Just off the coast, there were islands. Several islands, some smaller and one larger island… it read New Guinea. It didn't seem to have the same features of a coffee producing country… but maybe that didn't matter. More to the point, she seemed to be the type to like the refuge of an island. He raises his cup to his lips and takes a deep breath in. Assuredly, he turns around and becks, "New Guinea!". He looks at her to catch her looking at him with her jaw resting unclenched and her eyebrows meeting at the center of her forehead. "The Guinea pigs are self-aware." she says with the slightest crack of a smile.

Ben's smile crept up the side of his face, looking at her from the top of his eye sockets. He approached her with a line he had in his back pocket.

"Did you come here for the teas?" He says.

"I came here to spill the beans, but if you get me steamed, I'll roast them." She says.

"Wow that's dark, how long did you brew on that one?" says Ben

"It's well aged... but I fer-meant it." She says, looking him over.

" ...So, you fermented this coffee? I thought coffee was too acidic for the fermentation process?" Ben says

"Did you say Hasidic?"

" ..."

"I'm sorry this isn't a juice conspiracy." she laughs

"We are going nowhere fast." He says.

"You mean like old world lemons?... The only thing going nowhere is me with you." She replies

"Wow, sour much? Or just bitter?" He says.

"The next line out of your mouth better not be 'like your coffee' " She says.

"Ok. What's so special about this coffee?" He says.

"...You want the dirt? ...That's a secret." She says

"What do you mean?" He says

"The pith of it." She says

"The pith? "He says

She leans in and whispers, "The soil."

"...The soil?" He says

"Taste it again." She says

Ben takes a sip of it.

"What your tasting is called a terroir, it's from Earth Latin." She says

"For what?" says Ben

"Dirt." She says.

"It doesn't taste like dirt." He says

She smirks.

"I prime the plant to take on a certain kind of trait..." She says.

"What do you... what kind of trait?" He says

" A trait or..." She says

"Or?" He says

"Here." She hands him a business card with a name and number on it.

It read, "Tara's Future Coffee. Tara N. Fields. 555-555-555"

He turns to walk away and thinks to himself *At least I planted the seed*. Ben continues on his walk about the university, rubbing elbows with anyone he can, having the most favorable exchanges he's ever had. He's never been on a roll like this before. He settles reluctantly on the day, to be more reasonable about checking in on his roommate Max.

Chapter 2

MEET MAX, BEN'S ROOMMATE

Ben walks into the apartment to see Max with a thesaurus open on the coffee table evenly lined up with the tables edge, a calculus book open in one hand and the Xavier Chronicle in the other hand. This was typical of Max; one book was never enough. He seems to ignore Ben as Ben was carefully eyeing Max from the doorway.

"You coming inside?" Max asks.

"I thought I'd buy you dinner first." Ben says.

"Stop" Max says.

"I'm trying to wrap my head around this equation. Shh."

"I'll give you something to wrap your head around." Says Ben

"Try giving me peace for Thirty Seconds Ben!" Max says.

Ben tries to tip toe into the kitchen to grab sandwich fixings. He stacks on meats, lettuce and tomato inside the fridge and pivots to the counter.

"The dinner table is set. The counter is for food preparation and the cucumbers are done pickling. They're in a ball jar on the windowsill, near the cactus." Max says out of the side of his mouth without breaking eye contact with his book and paper.

"Oh, thanks Maximillian!... What are you reading about?" Ben asks.

Max calmly book marks his calculus book, sets it on the thesaurus and throws down the newspaper with a thwack! "Do you know what the Field's medal is?" asks Max.

"You know, I know what..." Ben starts.

"The Youngest PhD candidate, in Xavier, just nabbed it." Max says with a glare.

"What?! I thought you..." Ben starts again between bites of sandwich.

"Bounded Harmonic Functions. Ben, he blew me out of the water!" Max says.

"You mean he sunk your battleship?" says Ben choking down another bite.

"Don't start..." Max says.

"I'm not done. He sunk you before you could float your ideas about water tension variances?" Snarks Ben.

"Ben." Max pleads.

"Wait... Before you found out if they hold water?! PFFFFFTTT!!! *Spitting out bits of sandwich* Hahahaha! You've been at that longer than he's been a PhD candidate!" Ben sneers.

"Alright, Haz-Ben." Max retorts.

"Woooooaaah now buddy, NOBODY came close to predicting the supply chain boom of the Graphics Processor market like I did. I made more in two weeks than both your parents in their Lifetime!" Ben says.

"And you Still don't have this month's rent! Besides, you were the teacher's assistant to the pioneer of Hologram technology...." Max says.

"You know I'm good for it. A move like that took BALLS! What do you know about that? You recook your deli meats because you heard about ONE case of Banta Contagion." says Ben.

"It's a Flesh-Eating Bacteria BEN! it can eat through your throat, burst your jugular and bleed you out in 15 minutes!" Max retorts.

"Then why don't you just look at the meat first?" Ben says.

"Bacteria Ben... They're small." Max says.

"But you just said they eat meat; can't you See that?" Ben asks.

"Ok. Not doing this. Did you bring the yogurt or not?" asked Max.

"What yogurt?" asked Ben innocently.

"Ben, please don't tell me you ate it all... It was a Tub of yogurt." said Max.

"Okay do you want to dwell in the past or get a glimpse into the future?" Ben asks.

"Ben, you know I can't resist time travel... What is it?" asks Max.

"Just look." Ben says leaning over and opening his coffee cup.

"It looks like Tomato juice... What's so special about tomato juice?... Are you sneaking tomato soup out of the cafeteria again?" asks Max.

"That's the thing Max. It's not! It's Coffee!" Ben cheers.

"... Did you check the tamper seal on that yogurt?" Max says.

"Taste it." Ben says, shoving the cup to Max's gaping mouth.

"Great Scott! Ok!" Max says, cautiously taking a sip of it. His eyes widen. He takes another, and then downs the rest.

"Hey!" says Ben.

"This is not just coffee Ben; this is better than the brews I've tasted at monasteries! This terroir is Divine!" Max says.

"It's out of this world right?!" exclaims Ben.

"I've got this growing warmth in my belly... it feels... Comforting and at the same time Exciting... I Need to look at my notes again!" Max says running into his computer room to research.

Ben let's him get back to his "lair" so he can settle in and appreciate the fresh catch of business cards... He had one from a professor in the Anthropology department to find out where he gets his pants, the head of the Psychology department to ask him about his pocket watch, the manager of the Janitorial department to ask him about the dinner bell malfunction and the progress on the clogged toilets in the B and M halls, the number to his Calculus teacher's assistant because he's struggling with the theory of half-lives and radioactive decay, the business card to Tara's future Coffee Co-op, the number to the women's studies secretary for H.R. connections or as he referred to it " Human Relations", a member of the Anatomy and Physiology department to ask him about his strange mole, a student in the Audio Visual club about how to reserve presentation equipment, and the number of a girl in his Botany class because he can see a "budding work relationship".

The girl in his Botany class, Ivy, was an objectively beautiful woman, who happened to have a "cozy" relationship with his Botany professor. This put him in a preferred position. Ben was a sociable kind of person very approachable and charming. His eyes were a dark, inviting hazel brown. This worked favorably for a business major and botany minor. He locked eyes intently as he opened the minds of prospective future clients. These eyes beckoned the attention of any eyes they encountered. This applied to his interaction in a capacity with Ivy.

Ben woke up one day looking to see his recent friend, and confidant (Ivy). Ben was in Ivy's League. She'd be easier to talk to then Tara who was out of this world. He went ahead and called her after he tended to the throbbing in his head. He poured a coffee into his heated thermos and dialed in.

"Hello?" Ivy answered groggily.

"Good morning!" Ben says.

"Is this Ben?! It's been a while." She exclaims at attention.

"Yes." Ben says.

"Hold on Ben. I'm not even human right now. I'll call you Right back." She said.

click Ben shrugs and drinks his coffee. He looks at it with disappointment and adds some half and half from the fridge. *How does Tara do it? * He thinks.

Ben leans into the couch and picks up the Xavier Chronicle that Max left on the coffee table. The headline reads "Age No Factor in Field's Medal Formula". Ben keeps reading. "Rookie Dexter Rand is the youngest PhD candidate in all of Xavier University. Just two years into graduate school and already clenched the Field's Medal. No small feat for a 23-year-old, though not out of the blue. Paraphrasing from a meeting with his parents Ada and Paul, Dexter excelled in mathematics from a young age. You could always tell when he was working on a math problem because he would be flexing his fingers and touching them to his thumbs. He had a hand math system. His peers thought he might play guitar, as it also happened, he did. Dexter could play songs already written though, nothing more. He would occasionally throw a tweak on a note or two but was generally bound to the written work. Sometimes it was hard to tell if he was practicing a solo in his mind or calculating an equation. He was on the honor roll at his run of the mill high school and a seasoned winner at the brain game finals. When he took his SAT's and ACT, he set the standards for Mathematic scholarship. Dexter even Aced the Gaokao (The national Chinese collegiate entrance exam). It was no surprise that he was awarded the full amount by most colleges but Xavier's distinctive position in the field of mathematics made it an easy choice. As a bonus it was located on an off-world planet where some of his peers would say he belonged."

Chapter 3

MEET DEXTER

Dexter was approached in a study session for his advanced calculus class. Dexter, a double PhD candidate both in Theoretical Mathematics as well as Geology, forced himself to remediate and mingle with new students to keep him sharp and relevant. Some believe this was his subconscious desire to have company that he didn't have, estranged in his office. Dexter was considerably young, in fact, the youngest doctor in his field at Xavier. He graduated with his B.A. in Applied Sciences at a bright and tender age of 20. At the time, it was unheard of for someone that age to be accepted into graduate school, let alone go on to achieve a PhD in the field of Mathematics. He could transform any logic problem into a mathematical theorem; It was an uncanny feat and made him stand out in the mathematics classes he took.

It was no surprise to Dexter's mathematics professors that he would earn the Xavier Field's medal. He saw equations anywhere he set his eyes. It was a myriad of majesties that would unfold in his mind… but it took a sad toll on his personal life. He would rarely be surrounded by more than stacks of books or computer screens. He assembled an amazing collection of older computing machines to apply his genius and bring his cognition to fruition. He was out of touch with other students regularly. Ironically, his fingers where calloused from playing guitar and the handling and sorting of crystals. They imparted a brilliance to him. He had a kind of drive for their mysteries, that way, few could wrap their minds around. At the same time, something was eating at him, something that only constant study and applied science could quell. His office was a spectacular example that few ever had the chance to witness. He preferred isolation and fittingly his company was rarely sought until he met Ben. When Ben came into Dexter's class one day to sit in on his genius it would be fateful.

Chapter 4

IVY'S LEAGUE

Ben, having just finished the article on Dexter, gets a call from Ivy. *ringing*

"Big Ben speaking" Ben spoke.

"Ben Darius Oberman! What are you up to? Want to grab a coffee?!" Ivy exclaimed.

" I just had one, but I could go for a second round. "Says Ben

"Name the place."

"Ezra's. People have been raving about the new coffee there!" Ivy says.

Perfect. I'll pick you up around 11." Says Ben.

"Gotcha!" says Ivy*click*

This could be good; Ben thinks to himself. Ben looks to his wardrobe and picks out his loose-fitting hoodie and sweatpants, does a few pushups to get a little sweat, sprays on cologne, grabs his keys and leaves the room. Her dorm was in the Ballantine quadrant, so it wasn't far from the mess hall and a short walk to Ezra's. It wasn't more than a few blocks from his quadrant Tiberius. He rode in on his motorcycle anyway. It was an Anyong, made in Indonesia but people often mistook it for a Chinese bike called a Yin yang. He thought she might be able to see it from her window.

He walks all the way to the Levatron, in her building, and floats to the 4th floor

"Hey! is that your Yin Yang?" Ivy yells

"Actually, it's my Anyong, if you want to see my Yin Yang, I'll have to roll up my sleeves." Says Ben

So, he does and shows her the year-old tattoo of a Yin yang on his arm.

She smirks.

"You wanna ride?" He says,

"Yeah!" She says,

They ride the 4 blocks to Ezra's.

Ezra's was packed and buzzing with a fervor.

Ben could hear the conversations as he passed by groups with Ivy on his arm.

"It's incredible! She must be a genius! I need... "

"Her hair is so luscious..."

"I wish her coffee could..."

"She could be a star, but she just stays..."

" Shade grown? Maybe that's..."

"The ticket gets one coffee so I had to take my boyfriend's."

"Sticky fingers, it's got me looking for half-filled cups of…"

"Coffee? It's not just coffee."

Ivy looks over at Ben,

"What is going on? I've never seen this place buzzing like this!" Ivy says,

Ben veils a smile in reverie and says, " I don't know, but the brew here must be good!"

They get to the front of the line.

"My mom always told me to be wary of someone with hazel eyes." Ben said.

"Is that so?" Says Ivy.

Ivy gets to the coffee bar.

"I'll have a Hazelnut Coffee Freeze" says Ivy

"I'll have a Carmel Mercado with whip cream" says Ben.

They walk over to the business end of the coffee bar.

Ivy asks Ben, "What are you wearing? It smells great!"

Ben smirks and shrugs, "I don't know, it came in a gift basket from a startup debut I financed." Ivy melts a little under the gaze of Ben.

The work study barista behind the bar calls out Ben's name, makes eye contact, recognizes him, tilts her head and pushes his "Mercado" to him with two fingers. Ben frees his arm to stir his Mercado" completely nulling the point of having its shots poured over its foam. Ivy gets a wink and a smile from the barista. Ben wrangles her arm and makes a cool few steps to an open table.

"I've got the dirt on Tara and Project Pith. I saw you talking at The Jitter Bean." Ivy says.

"What's new on this front?" Says Ben.

"She harnesses the flavor using a specific jelly like material." Says Ivy.

"Jelly?" Says Ben.

"Sort of. She calls it a Super Scobie." Says Ivy.

"Scobie? Mysterious." Says Ben.

"It's basically germs. She calls it pre-germinants." says Ivy

"I've never heard of it. Tell me more." says Ben

"It's these germs she creates in a lab. She's very secretive about how she makes them. That's not all though. She uses them to alter the plants." Says Ivy.

"How could she do that?" Ben asks.

"I'm not sure exactly but if I'm going to dig any deeper, I'm going to need some assurance." Says Ivy.

"What kind of assurance?" Asks Ben.

"I want in." Ivy says.

"No." Says Ben.

"Look, this could get a lot more interesting if I get what I ask for. If not, it's on your hands." Says Ivy.

"Wait... ok. What exactly are you asking for?" Says Ben.

"I want to be on the ship. I'm Health Stat Technician certified with a specialization in urgent response." Says Ivy.

"Woah, how'd you know about the ship?" Asks Ben.

"..."

"Ok then, on one condition. You are not to be seen or heard from the others until we call for you from Rhea 7. You'll be a special request support member." says Ben

"Ok. Deal. Where's the flight plan transparency scans?" Asks Ivy

"Right here." says Ben

"Looks good then.? I'll get back to you next week." says Ivy

Whether it was right or wrong she left

Chapter 5

MEET LANDON

The final member of the team was Landon. Landon had a muscular build. He was raised in the farmland of Ectos, in the Pleiadean galaxy. He was very much a man of his time and place, a very humble farm man. He had an intimate knowledge of plant life based solely on experience. He had an intimacy with plants that rivaled Ben's taste of them. He wasn't the most classically intelligent one on the team by any means, but he wasn't the least inclined to perform. He was a tactile learner. He immersed his hands into everything he was doing, constantly engaging what he was interested in. He had more practice in earthly matters than any other crew member. Where they buried their noses in books, he plunged his hands into the soil and roots. He tended them. He even hand fed his livestock. A genuinely endearing character: he told tales, made jokes and had good taste in drink.

Though Landon worked as a janitor to pay his debts; he was the kind of person to find some amusement in it. Some days, for example, he found little abandoned pieces of other lives that he was privy to pilfer. One day, he'd been cleaning after the students and found a notebook.

The notebook Landon found, outlined a theoretical hydroponic apparatus. He noted to himself, that it lacked a practicality. At the bottom of the front page was a note that read "if lost return to dorm room 314 of the Ballantine quadrant." Being an honest Samaritan, Landon climbed the stairs to the Ballantine quadrant and knocked on the door of room 314. Max, shaken from his routine, huffed, and puffed to the door. Landon greeted him and told him that whether he liked it or not he had perused his notebook and found some errors. "His design was flawed". Ben was listening from the kitchen around the corner. He pivoted and said, "Why don't you come in and talk with us for a second?"

"Your schematics are precise, but they aren't fool proof." Landon said.

"What you're trying to do is make a Self-sustaining hydroponic farm, but you're forgetting something." Landon said.

"What's that?" Max said.

"You need to maintain it… You can't completely factor out the human element. The exactuated sluice for example. It needs lubricating and the gears will eventually degrade. One day they won't be able to move the water from ebb to flow." Landon said.

"How do you mean exactly? I can equate the function of friction into a time schedule of awareness cycles. The computers can monitor the patterns of flow. How about that?" Max replied.

"I think… what he means is that you are not said computer and we humans are inherently flawed. That translates to all human works." Ben said.

"More or less." Landon said.

"More specifically, the exactuated sluice. If you used a traditional rod bearing to move the sluice it would be easier to fix, it would have to be fixed slightly more often but it would be far more realistic for the man working on it."

Max was panting at the thought. "I don't need to imagine any trifles for my gadgets. They aren't toys they're brilliant." Max said.

"There's nothing wrong with a good plan. The Law of Murphy states that you must account for the unaccounted for and that's something you missed." Said Landon.

"I think you got yourself into a bargaining position*ring ring*. Hold on." said Ben.

"Who's that?" said Max

Chapter 6

LANDON EFFECT

Ben looks at the profile indicator. "It's Mary Jane, she probably just wants the notes from Botany class." Said Ben.

"Ok, you can just call this foolish but I think someone's got to tend to the equipment like we used to before computers took over." Said Landon

"You INCOMPUTE!" Max said.

"You can't account for those things because they're not your works!" said Max.

Ben steadied Max's hands with a cup of decaf.

"Max, listen. If Frank the farmer wants to work; why don't we give him something he can work out?" said Ben.

"My work?!" said Max.

"It looks like you've got your hands full." said Landon.

"Wait. Landon, do you like steak?" said Ben.

"I do." said Landon.

"I've got a hot tip on a bar that serves some of the best top sirloin in the city. First things first, would you like to discuss this over coffee before I take you to dinner?" said Ben.

"Sure." said Landon.

"I'll be in touch with you then." said Ben.

Ben invited Landon to coffee at the university mess hall and Landon, with an independent work schedule, accepted. It was 2:30 and the mess hall had better days. There were coffee cups strewn all around the café' with a leisurely care. "PhD candidates", Landon might have said. Ben was waiting in the corner of the café'. The seats had plushy arm rests and curves. Landon strolled out of the janitor's rear entrance, unbeknownst to Ben, and slyly snuck a seat next to him. Ben was trying feebly to catch the eye of the lone barista at the café register.

"You know she's not looking at you right?" Landon muttered out the side of his mouth.

"Where'd you come from?!" Asked Ben.

"I've got it in good with the league of janitors, they let me in ways around the school you'd never believe." Landon replied.

"Wait! She Was looking at me. She even winked." Ben said.

"Aria? She's got a wall eye; she probably noticed your stare and winced." Landon said.

"Oh, you've got a sense of humor too, huh? Do you always shoot down romantics with your sharp wit?" Ben said.

"Only when their barkin' at the wrong side of a fence." Landon said.

"…. So, how'd you find this job anyway?" said Ben.

"I used to play skee-ball with the president of the Janitor's union. He never was that good, but he bet me I couldn't beat him, and I upped the ante and told him he owed me a job if I did, and sure enough…." Landon said.

"And so, from humble skee-ball ambitions you fell into an even humbler Janitor career. I can see you're not intrigued by the trappings of fame." Ben replied.

"No, If I was into all that I would've entered in the skee-ball cup on Destiny planet. They've made a promise to the winner to be the game show host for a Televizi Show." Landon said

".... So, you spend a lot of time playing skee-ball?" Ben said.

"I split my time between that and reading the university journals of aspiring doctors. I make it a habit to keep my wits sharp and take it upon myself to send them letters reminding them they're human." Landon smirked.

"Is that a joke? You don't have a PhD." Ben said.

"No, I've got experience building farm equipment and had a lot of time on my hands before and after. I spent most of my downtime reading the manuals on the equipment and writing to the manufacturers when something broke." Landon said.

"That explains a lot. So, you could build one yourself then?" Ben asked.

"I've torn them apart every which way and put them back together again, all the techs and all the manual writers couldn't do it like me." Landon said.

"Where do you see yourself in ten years?" Ben asked.

"Playing skee-ball in a dive bar on Destiny." Landon said.

"How old are you anyway?" Ben asked.

"34 and change." Landon said.

"That's a bit higher than our average crew member but we could use some technical expertise. Do you really think you can eke out a meager living on janitor wages into your late 30's?" Ben asked.

"I never said I would keep this job, or even find another janitor job. I don't usually stick with any job that doesn't fluff my pillow, I'd say in the next two years I'd find some other bastard to beat in skee-ball and find myself on another planet working for another conglomeration." Landon said.

"I'm going to stop you right there and ask that you don't. I want you to sign onto our team. I've brought a contract and a space pen to get you signed up for duty." Ben said.

"Excuse me for this but I'm a little dumbfounded, I don't know anything about what you're doing there, who's funding the mission and what the pay, and job duties, would be like." Landon said.

"Landon those are fair questions, I might be a little excited, excuse me. The mission was written up by Huban Farms, a professor of Nuvo Terra Formae, Space Latin for New Earth forming. He wrote the outline here in this document you can read at this table."

Ben slid a packet of paper over to him. "It basically states the timeframe of reasonable use of the moon we will be setting up base, Rhea, and the solar revolutions we can expect to see before it has lost its hospitability and the subsequent launch to Andross. I was granted a commission, through Huban, by the space conglomerate Galactorb for finding the moon. I've also been awarded the position of oversight on Titan base 1 to oversee the budget's execution. Being that everything will be taken with us, we are to be paid in food for the mission and leisure time is included on the ship. We are being set up with the frontier elite's computer equipment, the very same that saw to the renovation of Gibbous on Rigel 7. We are allotted each, 100, 000 Galactorb credit units for deliveries and travel…"

"100,000 Galactorb credit units?!?!?! That's enough to pay the entire university for two years!!!" Landon exclaimed.

"…It's a lot, Landon because it is a very daunting task. I don't want you to think that any part of this mission will be easy. There will be free time of course, but this is a painstaking feat of science; nothing short of miraculous. There will be times when you will doubt the likelihood of our mission, but the credits are to ensure the faith in our project." said Ben.

Landon takes the contract off the table and rolls it into his grip and tucks it under his left arm. Ben eyes him soup to nuts and raises his chin to meet his look.

"You can't take that home with you, that's not how this works." says Ben.

"That's exactly how this works, I'm gonna sleep on it and get back to you in the morning". Says Landon.

"Landon, if you walk away from this table, with that contract, you walk away from this team." Says Ben.

Landon's eyes widen and his jaw opens to let out a bellow.

"I've got the right mind to use this contract as I see fit." says Landon.

Ben's mouth opens. Landon lunges the contract at him, and Ben sways and lifts the point of his pressurized pen to the tip of his lip. The contract stops short of his pen. Landon's foot is at the nearest leg of Ben's chair. Ben lower's the pen and his elbow catches a dowel rod an inch outside of its place in the lower backing of the chair. Landon lowers his rolled contract and Ben raises his right hand to grip the edge of the table. Tara, curious to see Ben in the quadrant café', peers around a corner and locks eyes with Landon and lashes flutter for a moment as Landon bends up his wrist, tilting the contract. Ben pushes against the table and his rear end slides back over the polished seat and pushes the lowest bar out of the spinal support of the chair. There's an audible thud and creek as the bar hits the floor and the two thick lengths of the spinal support start to split. Ben's posture repositions and he rounds up a few words for Landon, finger in the air now.

"Alright, Landon. Take tonight to think about your next move and I'll let you take home what you came for." says Ben.

"You'll have it tomorrow. Right, Landon?" says Ben. "Tomorrow" says Landon with a gleam in his eye.

The inside of the janitor's closet near the Ballantine quadrant was particularly well arranged. Landon was at home there. He never minded the wafting of steam in past the door. There was a series of vents. The higher vents bringing in cold air and the lower ones letting in the heat. The fan at the top center point of the ceiling ran by a switch at the entrance of the room. There was a faint buzz behind the walls. The beams, seated well in their place, provided passive support. The paper on the walls bubbled in places and the drywall beneath it acted as a thin barrier between the piping and the space inside the small room. It was a combination of the many elements of his life. His hours there were ultimately more productive than one could expect. The walls were reinforced by the same style of boards that ran along the floor. It was all but bare and wide to the eye, but it was also comfortable for the former farmer's son. It was at the bottom of the building where the light of most days never saw. The halls down there were a semblance to another time. Few men traipsed or lurked there and even fewer stood in any of them very long. They were smattered with paints and lacked a fine all-encompassing theme. The designs were bold and, on every surface, but the wet concrete at the foundation of the building.

Chapter 7

WHAT'S BREWING?

Landon makes it home, walks in past the door frame and inside his room. He brings the paperwork to his lounge chair and brings it under the light. Landon turns the pages past the contract. "Actuated Sluice" is in bold print at the very top of one of the pages. Landon lifts it and there is a litany of transparencies beneath. Each of them unveiling a more intricate design than the one before it. Ten sheets of which reveal a grand feat of engineering. Immediately followed by the equally intricate applications of the designs. Twenty more pages of diatribes on the same diagrams. Mathematic patterns totaling the sum of what could've been years of scholarly work. It wasn't just the contract… Landon's surprise surfaces and lifts to reveal some intrigue. Ben pawned off Max's work with the team contract. He probably thought he had a bargaining position. That's rich. It would take Landon the whole night to make sense of it.

It was getting into the evening and Landon had to decide what he was going to do. In a flash, Landon decides he'll take it to memory to double down on this new ambition. Landon looks at his watch. It's ten fifty-two. He goes to a drawer, by the entrance of his room, and pulls a faucet out of it. He throws his hand through the adjacent wall and wraps it around a lead pipe. There's a small knob just above his hand, he twists it and steam wisps out. He wrenches the section beneath it off and switches it out with the faucet. He tightens it up quickly and nimbly nudges the knob above it. He throws himself to the shelf within his reach and grabs a ceramic mug by its handle. Landon puts the mug under the attached faucet and releases the valve. Piping hot water fills his mug. He reaches to the second shelf and grabs a can of coffee grounds. He opens it, pours 3 ounces in it and rests the mug of coffee on the third shelf to brew. Landon liked his coffee thick.

Meanwhile, back at Max's, it's eleven o clock and Max is waiting for his mind to turn off. Every light is dimmed, every appliance at a low hum, and 3 out of 9 light bulbs, still on, were casting a color scheme over him. His attention is scattered, though his mind is not. Elegant in its categorical genius. Unique and intrinsically qualified to appreciate itself. Undeniable potential actuated in physical form so obvious to its beholder that not a one could be made more aware. The amplitude of the inner cognition intensified and imparted a series of brilliant flashes in his brain. Equidistant was the filament in the nearest bulb.

The quandary was this: "Where did my transparencies go?" the answer was obvious, but it didn't keep him from questioning. Each answer birthed more questions. It was a personal conversation he could get deeper in each consecutive second for as long as he had a resistance to entropy. It was one query after another. Of course, there was an end in mind. He knew he would have to wake up the next day and put himself to work, but it was not nigh, and definitely not his first thoughtful night. His attention came back to his well-conceived work. Designs ad infinitum. Mathematics that led beyond the usual human limits. It wasn't the most important piece of work he'd ever made, but it was widely appreciated for its furthering of the current science of the time and deep creativity. A select kind of people had witnessed it and now it had a new observer somewhere and it was particularly disconcerting.

Max had appreciations few had garnered in any similar way, but there was one. One younger man that had gotten seemingly as close but with much less ado. He'd taken fewer steps. Trudged through far fewer murky mires than Max. It was notable. Actually, much more noteworthy than he cared to admit, and it was unreasonable to assume he'd fall short of his own accomplishments. The man was astounding, and it was increasingly bewildering. Lauded. He was lauded. Landon on the other hand was possibly the humblest man Max had ever met. It was a tough assessment to make, but an accurate one. He didn't know many in the whole of the university that could understand and recite his works as well. Max appreciated that. It was endearing. It wouldn't take him long to understand what the schematics were meant to build, if it was him who had them, and it would feasibly take him a short time to create a replica. Landon was strong, capable and fierce. It was up to him, what would become the next phase of this operation. Max could tell it was in his cards and well within his reach.

Chapter 8

DEXTER REVISITED

At the Auriclestle quadrant, in a previous time, in the primary wing of the university, there was a boom in intellectual achievement. At the forefront was a young man by the name of Dexter Rand. An intellectual endowment recipient and a contender for several fellowships. He was an impressive youth with nearly universally acknowledged potential to a profession. There was an acceptance that came with the kind of notoriety he had acquired through his scholarly achievements. He was at the top of his class and a heavy weight in the Theoretical Mathematics Department. Dexter wasn't overqualified to be a student by any means, but he was nearly nuclear in the kind of brain power he possessed. It was a sight to behold whenever he was at the chalkboard at the front of the classroom. He was as quick as he was thorough. Every equation meticulously ascribed to a theorem he'd conceived of. Whether or not they were pure of origin was a mystery held only to him.

Dexter was a mathematician's wonder. He was an embodiment of exceptionalism. He was unmatched in his class each day. It was entirely impressive to the people that bared witness. It was unbearable for the ones that held their heads so very dear to their hearts though. He put them to shame. Theory was a cold science to him in many ways. Apart from the luke-warm heart he kept in his chest. His achievement garnered hubris. His works weren't devoid of consequence, and he knew that, but at the same time, they were celestial, though Earthly in that consequence. His thought process was often unconsciously speaking to the ones who could grasp it. It nearly imbued a kind of potential onto those of which who could take it at it's true worth. Alien to many but that was the fascination of it. It was almost a connection to other worlds and on the planet of Xavier University, that meant a great deal.

As a talent, he was scouted often by several very large conglomerates, agents specifically. Notable conglomerates being: Geodonna, Leucadio and Lumocorp. Hinuz had even rang his number a few times after their rampantly successful pharmaceutically infused line of Catchoops in 3139. The specific effects of which incurred a notable condition called "Tomacular Rosacea" which imparted a distinct hue to the perspective of the human consumer. The advertisements were a spectacle and well known in their successive broadcasts. Each progressively more impressive and alluring. The captivating qualities were hard to pinpoint, but they aired for two Xavyears. A long time to any federated Planetian. In that same time, Dexter had accrued the interest of 8 vertically owned corporations.

Dexter was an enormous credit to the university. His efforts were converting more followers to larger edifices that cast broad shadows over his quadrant. Days passed relatively slowly in comparison to the central galactic time zone of Earth, but also in duplex. There was a larger and smaller sun casting even amounts of shine over Xavier. One was closer and one was farther. The light that shined past the other onto Xavier was had a formula of which Dexter had posited, in its relativity, garnering a preferred status to its creditor.

Dexter had a very valuable skill set. The technical term for it was "Quant". It was an industrial term for people who possessed extraordinary mathematical processing power. He was a grade above the rest, and it was quite clear. This made offers aggressive and bold. He was often tangled in the many, would be, strings, but he was studied and there was someone who understood that about him. That person was a lower-level affiliate of a speculative ventures corporate entity. There were many like him, but he was humbled more often than the rest. He was diligent but partially tasked with heavy stacks of paperwork. One of the stacks he was tasked to was a written proposition for Dexter, which he'd come to understand through his published work. This man had a kind of access that wasn't his alone but an advantage none the less. He accessed the large file and arranged the referential footnotes in another order; course correcting Dexter's trajectory.

Chapter 9

FLASH FORWARD

In a more recent time, while the crew was having a round table, Dexter was compelled to walk to the "lonely" stream a mile off campus. It gave him a chance to stay with his thoughts. His day was lacking something he couldn't quite place. The feeling hung over him like a fog. The stream was there for a semblance of comfort. There wasn't anything natural about it. It carried sediment from the power plant nearby, and eerily affected the transplanted fish in the pond it fed into. He'd heard stories of people catching workers reseeding the pond with fish every few weeks, but in his state, it didn't mean much. One of Xavier's moons shone a light over these fish that gave them a hue.

    The fish were busy sucking up muck and nipping at each other. They might never know anything else. The muck, though, had its own deposits, shining at the shallow end of the pond. The fish never strayed far from them. They were like lamps in their foyer. It was strange and beautiful. Not a single thing out of place, and yet one could be plucked up from it. They'd swim the same. Unencumbered by gravity like himself. It was a novelty. A piece of their little ecosystem. A treasured modern artifact. So, he rolled up one sleeve and reached in. It came up from the muck rough, but with a lather it shone like it had underneath the water. It was a familiar clarity with a frosted appearance on the inside. looking closer he could make out what looked like a kind of pattern. An unnatural pattern. He looked through it to the moon in the distance and within it was a litany of light. A moments' majesty beheld. It didn't lend itself to him easily like most things. Something there like a spark. On the off chance he could make it to the university before the doors closed, he took it and left. The mile before him was short with his sights set a little higher. The shadows less ominous than they'd be when the doors closed at 10.

The double doors creaked as they swayed and the lumens of the fluorescent bulbs above him had him wince. The geology wing still had the lights on. The equipment was covered and cabinets closed. He walked in and set the crystal at the metal working table. The microscope and the laser attached would provide the view into this small wonder.

Chapter 10

WHAT'S COOKING?

The morning after the round table, Ben wakes up with a pounding in his head. He can feel matted sweat in his thin wispy hair. He lifts the bed cover off his chest and folds it into his waist. Looking up, he stares at the center of the fan in his room. A factory-made fan. There was likely one just like it in every other room in his quadrant. The cool air, that drifted down to him, was what was important. It was pleasant and entirely refreshing to his flushed face. His ribs expanded and contracted with ease as his lower lungs made way for air to fill him up. Not an incredible feat of science, common, but less measurable, then the pressure in his veins. He turned his head to the cracked door. The less natural light that beamed in opposed to the sun's rays; shone through the windows. It was a blunt light, one that was muted a bit more than the light through his blinds. It was welcoming almost certainly. In the way a lesser light is in the presence of a blinding light.

Ben threw the cover off and swiveled his legs over the side of the bed and he put both feet down. Hands on his knees, he looked up and sighed and stood. He walked to the door, opened it wide and continued walking to the kitchen, grabbing Max's daily paper off the coffee table on the way. Ben walks over the glass tiles and to the cold pressure dispersal unit called Afreya for short. He opens the door on it and finds a ball jar. Assuming the liquid in there is ethanol, Ben turns and releases the lid and tips the jar to his mouth. As it dispersed over his tongue, he realized it was a different yeast waste, not the product he was looking for. He swallows the remainder in his mouth, and it refocuses his attention from his head to his stomach. To his bewilderment, it gives him a fresh inwardly clean feeling. Not upsetting, but not wholly pride inducing either.

    Ben pivoted and then looked to the stove for the ceramic skillet he'd anticipated Max had left there. A few onions were above the overhead fan. He motions to grab them and brushes the on switch. There's a humming now growing louder and a dynamic kind of static feeling permeating his stomach. The emanation ripples through to his muscle tissue and undulates it. His pores start to spread, and his hair straightens up. The air current starts to wind under the fan and the draft, from the cracked window, is making its way to the brunt of the stove top. Vapor is wafting up from the middle of it. His hand on the knob of the cabinet, caught in a subtle stupor, it opens, and a flask falls cap first toward the awning above the stove. It slides down it and crashes to the ceramic skillet fracturing it into several large geometric pieces. The contents of the pint guzzle out steadily and within a moment's breath, the ether claps like thunder. Each of the ceramic shards thrust outward. The ether now engulfing every surface, within a 2- foot radius. Ben's eyelids shudder and his spine stiffens sending a jolt down his legs to his heels.

Chapter 11

TARA'S WAY

Tara, in her own way, had a revel worthy night. After the meeting she'd felt strangely beleaguered. She'd had her fill, and by the time she'd made it to bed, she'd felt even heavier. There was a real deep imbuing sense to her body. It was fitting she'd be in the dark for a while, brooding. There was, in part, an anxiousness that she couldn't handle easily with simple comforts. She was holding on by a string. Plugged into reality. Leaning on her strengths. It was the kind of thing she did. She wasn't all that surprised by how life happened. It wasn't for her always. The night grew longer as it passed. The depths within her growing. The drawer in her stand held a book, a new one she hadn't read before. It was something in a different light now. Something with wisdom, and a personal physical connection. It wasn't the furthest thing she could reach, and it was blunt enough that it could make its way to the door if someone intruded. It rocked in her palm from left to right, and just an hour before dawn, she opened it. With both thumbs on opposing sides of the open book, she looked at the written pages. The two pages in front of her were written in golden ink.

She was swept up in work the morning that followed. She couldn't quite follow up with the other 4. Her work study had an element that others didn't. She had a stake in the geology department and some in the agriculture department. There were a few halls she couldn't easily get into like the others, but she was inclined to sneak around them at odd hours. She'd found a few things interesting here and there. She was quite distinctly skilled at getting where she needed to be and in the order she'd prioritize. When the university clock chimed at noon, she'd had her passage through the halls. There were a few places she could walk to that would offer solace. It was a beautiful day, and it was pouring over the clouds falling in plain gold hue in front of her. There had to have been a minimum of 30-40 people under each auspicious arbor. The less that treaded the concrete, the less she had to make her way through. She could see glints off the eyes of her peers, and it offered her some due thoughts about a couple of very beautiful things.

One thing struck her within the instant. Her cycle was chained up and the key to the lock on it wasn't in her pocket. She'd have to find a ride if she planned on getting to her place in time to catch the hologram special, she'd planned on watching. Her bed seemed like a cot to her now. She'd get there, and quickly. There wasn't a short way about it. Then KABOOM! There was smoke starting to billow from Max and Ben's quad by the time this dawned on her. She'd gotten a quick look before she decided it might be a bad idea to stick around. She wasn't the only one who'd gotten the idea and she knew how it would work out if she'd just got one more look and moved on. It happened with a quickness. And instantly, she felt an arm under hers. She reacted with a swift knee and ran. Along her jaunt she checked a guy and grabbed the hand he reached out with, guiding him to the bike. She threw her shoes, he pulled up his sleeves, and they threw themselves at the bike.

The guy grabbed the key and Tara stepped back. Students knew how to mobilize when they had to, there was hope for humanity. He got on and she threw herself at the back. He just yelled "I got you" and she wrapped her arms around tightly.

It was a very fast bike. The hands he had on the bars were gripping tight. Her arms were like rope around him, cutting off his lower supply of blood. She was pinning her neck to his back and looking for some kind of response team behind them. The distance was widening, and the billowing smoke was rising. The G's she was feeling tensed her neck. The wind was rustling her hair in front of her face. The light behind the smoke was making patterns. The lesser light on the inside and the greater light above. It seemed like a scaling feat for fireman. Few had the ability to get to it at the pace it was burning. Still further, they were advancing to the outer edge of the catastrophe. The buildings seemed to lean in to the two as they sped up. Glass shining the sun in their direction. Ahead of them was a jam they'd have to make it through and a bridge that much farther.

The guy knew he'd be stopped if he didn't slow down. He lowered the gears and let the clutch take some heat off the brakes. The bike was an older model, that wouldn't be appreciated in pieces. He knew it would be important to maneuver it. He took it out of gear and skid to a stop. Hand still on the brake, he put his finger on the front air compressor switch and let off some pressure. The tires were hot and already showing wear. When they came to a standstill, they left a mark. The guy looked around tilting his head. The jam was this: flashing lights above the intersection, bomb squad heading in their direction. His jacket felt a little tight around his neck, but his stance was open. Tara on the other hand was looking up over his shoulder to update her situation. There was an immediate and dense pressure at the sides of her head. She was looking at an intense, ominous force of nature. A cold front was coming in...

Chapter 12

THE FIRE

At the same time, a sprinkler over Landon's cot was on full spray at noon, to Landon's alarm. Landon, groggy but not ill equipped, woke to this new personal storm. At full attention, he threw his bed cover and thrust himself to his feet. He was familiar with this kind of situation and knew exactly what he was going to have to do. He lunged to the wall and grappled the hook holding his tool belt to the wall. Wrapped his waist with it and fastened it. The wrench at his left came off well enough. He screwed the wrench's adjuster to meet the fitting size for the sprinkler, applied the force necessary and the line from the wall to his ceilings plugged... Pants were next, then the successive rows of pipelines down the hall from his room. The size of the heads on them would warrant a massive wrench. Landon had just that, behind a small door, in his room. He'd have to make use of it, and the smaller wrench, with a quickness. The knob to the hallway bent at the sudden shift and the door lurched open. Landon grabbed the long wrench and leaned it against the wall.

Pants, shirt, shoes, raincoat. Now at the ready, Landon muscled the large monkey wrench under his arm and **hustled** out the door. There'd be a lot of heads to turn. The lights over the mist gave a hue though the humidity in the hall. Landon barreled down, seeking the right pipe. The first of four in his range was just past a corner he could make out from his vector. Facing him it glistened as much as the light above it could impart. It was a main nut as big as his head. Passing lights gave him tunnel vision but he remained focused. Wrenches at the ready, he skids to a halt and affixed the smaller wrench to the bolt holding it in. Whipping the larger wrench, he met the main nut with a clang. Rust dropped off at the seating. He rolled the adjuster over the wall to gauge the right size and clasped it on. The force it called for required a shoulder to lever and a boot. He put his boot to the bolt wrench and with a bounce the nut wrench pivoted 20 degrees. There was a deep thud and a resounding howl. The first quadrant, now in for relief, gave him a moment to catch his breath.

Chapter 13

WATERLOGGED

On the same day at 1, Dexter woke up drenched. It could've easily been sweat, but it wasn't. He was soaked from head to toe. Even his shoes were thoroughly wet. He would be surprised if it weren't for the dripping sprinkler just above. There was a lapse in thought, longer than he was used to. He looked over to his Televizi and it dawned on him in waves. His eyes shifted to the coffee table. The Hologramatron was smoking. He threw his arm at it, and it fell back over the side of the coffee table. Flickering a luminescent vision of the last quartz disc within it. A project he'd been attentive to, but capricious with. A passion project you could say. He flirted with it nightly for weeks. In and out of a sort of passion. His heart was in it. Now, it was smoking on his floor, in one piece. His face didn't quite capture his frustration and astoundment. He reached over to it, frazzled, and rocked it, cradling it in his arms. He touched the disc spinner and pivoted the quartz. It was salvageable but the energy it required to realize it was debilitating. It wouldn't take a week. It could take a month, maybe more. It wouldn't be flirtatious anymore, it would be a pursuit. It was going to be an ornament for a while, while he looked at the damage in his room.

Dexter's term paper, on his quantum computer was a total loss. His guitar, with the enamel on it, would need to be polished. He went to it, looking it over. Its angle lent him a clue. It held water. He picked it up. It moved like a buoy. In his stupor, he sat down with it. He laid his fingers on the frets, picked a chord, and played it softly. It echoed almost. There was a beautiful sound. It was like the ocean was calling him. He could hear a melody over it. It cooed him. He positioned his fingers in a C. He strummed it. then an F. He strummed that too. Then an A. He wept. It was too much. All his work, in shambles, and the only thing that held him together would warp. He couldn't bear it. He couldn't adjust. It was breaking him. He was fractured...

Chapter 14

BEN'S BENDER

Ben scrambles and hits his head. Max wakes up to the clamor with his air tank on (for better sleep to dream of genius). They both must get out of there before it reaches his oxygen tank. Max has the where with all to get Ben out of the room and into the hall. The fire is serious. Max, prepared for fire drills, takes Ben, along with everyone else, to the escape tube to land on the ground floor. After taking Ben to safety, Max realizes and calms down reassuredly remembering that his most valuable works are backed up in the university's archives. Ben is a little delirious from smoke inhalation and maybe a concussion. He just says the most absurd things to Max. Things that don't make sense.

"I am a part of the fire" he says.
"We need the smoke…"
"They couldn't pass this out."
"Why can't I be flame-retardant?"
"Nothing is anymore…"
"It spreads like thirst on a desert…"

"We could drink from the sand."

Max didn't know what to make of it, but Ben refused to go to the local hospital. Sacral Hearth. He wouldn't give a sensical answer, he was just vehement. It came out as,

"They'll have me then. They'll have me. They'll have me. I can't recover from the debt. It's dome high!" said Ben.

Max interjects, "Why don't you call Ivy then?"

He perks up.

"Ivy?! Yes, yes, yes." So, he calls Ivy, and she tells them to meet quickly. They get there and Max is let in on a little bit of something that he had no previous idea about. Background structure of the university and its ins and outs to governance. It was purposefully smoke and mirrors and cloak and dagger. Funding seemed derivatives based, and murky. The derivatives were based on the economy and the counterbalances seemed to be entirely based on the corporate credits exchange. It was so complex, but he kept gushing information. Max was entranced, but he couldn't shake the possibility that the smoke inhalation made him incoherent and a little confused. Ivy arrives and helps him to a bed and he falls asleep.

Chapter 15

FIRE BRAND

Landon puts out the fire finally and makes it down the scorched hall. While walking, he gets pulled aside by the chairman over the maintenance department who happened to be the Botany professor. The University structure allowed for cross monitoring for it to work like that. The botany professor, Huban Farms, grabbed him and started with a congratulations.

"Job well done. We knew we hired you for a reason. but I must be blunt. We need someone else to handle the press for this incident." Said Huban

"What we need you to do is go relax somewhere for a while, while this blows over. What do I get for handling this? A bonus! A very generous bonus. That comes with discretion. We need you to be discreet. Go home for a while and just relax." Landon is curious and has justly merited janitor privileges, so he uses them. To find the origin of the fire before the fire crew got there. He's quick and finds it's Max and Ben's room. It's a little alarming and finds it suitable that he lay low for a while. Landon goes home to his little closet apartment and has a couple of beers to relax.

Time passes and he turns the televizi to the university channel and there's already live coverage. Huban Farms is speaking in front of the camera, and it seems scripted. "It was an electrical fire. We've warned our students to keep the minimum number of appliances plugged in for this reason. We've contained the incident thanks to our regular fire drills and our effective sprinkler system." Landon is inquisitive. It's plausible but they didn't make mention of the origin, or him, for that matter. It might follow sense for anonymity reasons, but the electrical fire explanation was a little farfetched as he'd recently fixed the wiring on that floor. It was odd. Just then Max calls him.

"Have you heard the news?" Max said.

"I'm watching it right now." said Landon.

"Ben and I headed to a friend's house to cool off while this media circus rages on." Max said.

"Ben's a little worse for wear. His friend Ivy's been hospitable. She says your welcome. Why don't you come on over?" said Max.

"Alright, I've got some things I'd like to tackle with you two anyway." Said Landon

He comes over and talks with Max about what happened. Max tells Landon about what Ben said and tells him his head was injured. Landon sticks around to see How Ben would wake up. Ivy reassures Max and Landon that he should be okay if he doesn't fall asleep. While they're talking, he does though, and he wakes up with no memory of it. They are then gathered around him and insist he's fine. They fill him in, and Landon is a little leery. Ben plays it off well and they can tell he'll be well enough to get along from there. Ben then tells Landon and Max that he'd like to have a one on one with Ivy, just to make sure he's coherent and refilled in.

"You really don't remember the fire?" Said Ivy.

"No, I don't." Said Ben.

"I do, you're fine," Said Ivy.

"They said it was an electrical fire," Said Ivy.

"You're cleared." She reassured Ben.

"Consolidated Conglomerates of The Republic picked up the tab for our space mission." Said Ivy

"They rendered the ship today using Max's schematics." Said Ivy

"We're going to bankshot off Rhea to the Space Fold. From there we'll port through to Andross." Said Ivy

Chapter 16

LAUNCH TO RHEA

The ship was being loaded all morning, giving Ben the chance to sleep in. Landon, though, took it upon himself to see what they were loading. He could see mega machines for tilling, and he could just barely read the sign on a huge shipping container that read S.O.U.P. That wasn't the only cargo. There was a large cylinder that was spelled S.K.A. Landon had his janitor badge on, so he flashed it to the guy doing inventory. "Can I check for the sanitation equipment?" Asked Landon. The manager type let him look at the inventory. It was jam packed with acronyms. Though Landon couldn't miss the four-letter acronym for his sanitation equipment- Servile Human Instant Terralous, "S.H.I.T." Landon got to kind of skim the rest of the inventory. It seemed legitimate enough. Landon was curious about the S.K.A. and the S.O.U.P. but the inventory manager was holding that paperwork. He noticed Landon's curiosity and prompted him to "ask Ben", if he had any questions, deadpanning him. "We Launch tomorrow, get to the distal orderator and we'll just warp space around you and the team ordering your placement and suitedness in the time-space ,near field, renderer."

He did, and everybody got on Ben's level. Jarred by being disambiguated and then reiterated in this reality. The journey itself was relaxing and brief as these things could be semi arbitrarily sped up.

Time Quake

Chapter 17

THE STAY IN RHEA

Rhea was a moon of Jupiter it was a beautiful vantage to Jupiter's chaos and Saturn's rings.

Which segued nicely into conversation when Landon prompted Tara to look.

"Look at these chaotic worlds granting us a purview of their majesty. I remember looking at pictures of them and now we get to look at their grand chaos in full resolution... They're nearly as curious as you. Deeply active in the layers of surface and radiant with potential." Said Landon.

Tara bent to his gravity and let him pull her folded arms to his chest and they embraced.

Time Quake

Ben was working with Max on the ship's sensors. There were a lot of features they weren't quite familiar with. Though, there was a manual and it seemed Dexter was obsessively studying it while Max was harmonizing the equipment. The ship was intuitive but unusually so.

Max finished up syncing and harmonizing the equipment through its interface. Dexter wasn't looking good. He was secluded and muttering to himself. Max had seen this before and had Ivy watch over him through the ship's cameras. She relished it. Ben had administered access to the ships management protocol. Dexter's muttering seemed to be a song of sorts. The ship had some auxiliary protocols. Ben turned them on to approach Ivy. Ivy whispered to Ben, "This might be the right time to launch the S.K.A." Dexter then started screaming.

"Tests! We're all guinea pigs to Conglomo!" said Dexter.

Dexter then ran to the ship's control room, but the ship shielded the room by protocol. Ben had overridden Max's harmonizing to bolster the defense of the control room. Ben then ordered a cell for Dexter.

Time quake

Ben tells max to launch the terraforming equipment a little early while Tara and Landon were in Tara's quarters. Ivy sees the two and leans on the controls to face Ben and launches the S.O.U.P. Max doesn't think that's right and looks up what it is, and it stands for Scobie of Universal Purpose. It lands on Andross and drills deep into the planet-like moon. The terraforming equipment then gathers around it, beginning their automated work. Max yells for Tara for reference. Tara throws on her uniform and runs to the camera room.

Ivy whispers, "We launched your little product."

Tara blows up."That wasn't supposed to be for 3 more cycles! *adjusting her bra strap* You're going to ruin it! It had to be carefully introduced!" *It was alive after all*

"You're going to kill it!" screamed Tara.

Time Quake

Dexter is in isolation humming an eerie tune and laughing to himself

Chapter 18

"YOU'RE BREAKING UP"

The strangely flowering plants were ready to be harvested. The dome home was ready too and the air conditioning was perfect. The place had a little furnishing made of a very comfortable plush. The harvest was for the return to planet Xavier but they could take some under the guise of testing. Ben smoked the strange hybrid flower and started hallucinating. Ivy seized this opportunity to talk to him and get him to sing his harmonic into the management protocol for a drink. Meanwhile Max found some buried paperwork on the business model and mission statement of the creditor to the mission. Ben had that role in the team, and it reeked of arrogance. The crediting was run through a shell company Ben set up through Huban Farn and it funneled all the profits. Andross was also explicitly stated to be a slave colony and Ben planned on managing it from the ship. Max brought this to Tara and highlighted a contingency plan written for Ben that stated an explosion to erase all traces of this enterprise if it went awry. Tara ran to the control room where a drunk Ben was eyeing the detonation button.

Space Apples

The S.O.U.P. had taken to the planet, and Ben was simmering on his jealousy of Landon. Tara could see it.

Tara probed Ben. "What are you doing, drinking in the control room?"

"I'm just thrilled that you and Landon have all you need. You know I'm just happy you don't need anything, from me." Said Ben

"I don't even know why I'm here." Said Ben

"I just wish I was innocent again, young and loved. Like you." Said Ben tearing up a bit.

There was a time dilator that was used to reorder the ship's contents like an undo protocol.

Ben threw his drink and dialed in the Time dilator and turned it on Tara. You could then see Tara live out her life in reverse, her body flying all over the ship and then balling and unballing from the fetal position to standing. While she shrunk, Ben stopped the dilator. Tara had turned back into a child. Landon, who had followed Tara, watched all this in horror from the entrance to the room. Landon ran over to Ben and body checked him into a shuttle pod.

"You will live to regret that!" Landon said as he pushed the launch button sending him to Andross. Ben though, still had a com link, so Ben harmonically ordered the ship to stay in orbit.

Ben said," This is my ship no matter where I am."

"We're not your ship!" said Landon.

Landon picked up Tara. He knew the sort of mechanics for the harmonizing protocols and the time dilator. Landon would fix this, and he could do it with songs. Landon started playing them from a controller he had with him, and Ben faded out of existence. While Tara seemed trapped in time. Landon played his swan song and slipped into time as well, beside Tara. The controller went haywire. Max merged with the control room; Ben turned into AI. Ivy grew old. And Dexter remained rocking back and forth, laughing, where they sequestered him. Landon and Tara would be looped for all time side by side, living, and reliving their whole lives, while Andross bred life, and the ship becoming Ben, would steadily provide oversight. Life on Andross was just beginning, but it's automated oversight would bring the recreation of the team in a strange math only Dexter had a clue about. The ship, and the planet would haunt that sector like a ghost mobile in a museum. Abstract art for an unknown observer on a distant dwarf planet-like moon called Andross.

LOVE FROM ABOVE

A disillusioned Hollywood dark horse, who happens to find some market research anomalies for her show, takes her liberty to track them down to one viewer. As a writer, she falls victim to her own imagination of a romantic premise to a rebellious, power dynamic, role reversal. Compelled by intrigue, she decides to use her status as leverage to satisfy her curiosity about this person. In her pursuit, she gains access to backdoors, tools, technologies, and channels. Adventure, and romance, ensues.

Fae feels like she lives in a fishbowl. Her life seems fake. She's aching for a reality, a realness. She's a producer on her show and that comes with perks. It's an internet show, so she gets to tool around with new market research.

Subconsciously, she's looking for something beyond ratings. She filters her audience based on what other shows they like on the website, until she finds one that likes all the shows she likes. SVU, SNL, The Outer Limits, and noticed his profile is rated for double the Nielsen tv ratings. She snoops a little bit and finds an icon that lets her see his market information compiled from his internet use. She's compelled by it. He's smart, politically active, and an aspiring writer. The peak into his life compels her to dive deeper.

She finds another icon, on her marketing suite of software, deeper in her search. The icon says: "The Outernet".

She clicks it and a fuzzy wave washes over her and saturates her brain. She can suddenly, intuitively, control the files. She uses the intuitive controls to open up her subject's camera. He's just watching tv, but she feels like he's watching her. He's actually watching her show. She feels like they're talking, but neither of them are using their voice. His eyes are just moving between items and characters on the screen. She intuits a question to her computer, and it answers by allowing her to influence the picture on his screen. The computer runs a render through so many filters you couldn't be sure she had any effect, but it was there. She raised her eyebrows at him and it rendered.

His eyes widened a second. He was more receptive than other people. His host like awareness, and forum to voices, called to her like an open stage. She reached out into the screen to touch him and his eyes widened. She used her spirit to open the window with his picture and she could see the room he was in like she was there. It was like augmented reality. He was unusually aware of the effect, like any other effect of psychosis. He was aware where the average wouldn't be. In some ways, it made him realer than reality.

She saw a pill bottle on his nightstand. It was an antipsychotic. This just added a dimension to her admiration, he was a witness to the otherworldly, and that qualified his treatment. She craved his realness. With her status, and tools, she could order him anyway she wanted, but she noticed something else, she could directly affect him.

She could feel his presence and putty-like potential in her hands. He was young and full of all that extra youth that made him so ripe. She could mold and shape him. She was going to reinvent him.

She spent the luxury of her free time watching him secretly. She spent so much so, that she felt connected more and more deeply to the window into his life. It was merging with her own life. When she was away, she could sense when he was watching her on screen. When she watched him, she felt assured.

One day the Outernet icon appeared in the corner of her eye, in her room this time. She felt a presence with it. She could open it intuitively again, and when she did, it became picture in picture. Over time, she began to lose herself from her original context. It had transformed. It wasn't simply curiosity anymore. It was something else. It was all consuming. She was beginning to see his world. A world no one else could see or believe in. She had a sort of membership to it. It was novel, so she played coy, watching him live his life with a double dose of reality. It was alluring.

Nowhere else in her world could she see this new dimension. Nowhere else had more life than what he was living, and he was alone in it. It was endearing. He was noble. He was navigating something new every day. Ironically, his life became her show. She'd watch him in it. She was inspired, touched, and enthralled by its complexity; and all the while, he'd watch hers. She didn't just want to stay in touch with reality, like others in the industry, she wanted to be consumed by it, she wanted it inside her, like it was inside him.

Outside and in, the other world weaved through his life, and no one could know, but her. She began to romanticize it. She saw the plain story like qualities, and as a writer and an actor, she eventually couldn't keep herself from it. She had to engage it. She had to be apart of it.

She started small. Just seeing if she could hint at things to him, highlight things, guide him. Like an angel. Imply messages of importance. Gradually, that lost its appeal and he wouldn't do the things she wanted, so she leaned on her membership to his mind. She wanted to be realer to him.

The division between her and the technology blurred. She was slowly becoming the "ghost in the machine". Musing him through his favorite songs on passing radios. Leaving love notes in the form of paranormal evidence. Her frustration with him and her power over him started to change how she interacted with him. She came to see him like an object, which wasn't much different then how surveillance capitalism saw him, but she was less rehearsed in it.

She began to see what rules she could break, and broke them. She began to curate his life, trying to set precedent, that would merit its legitimacy, trying to push the envelope. She wanted to bring it all to life, bridge the gap between worlds. She had ideas all her own. Ideas of what he should do and what he should be, like a character on her show.

She began alternating between love and control. She'd croon for him at times, other times she'd guide, but that wasn't enough. Her frustration manifested and she became aggressive. That extra slice of pizza, no. That walk to the store, no. That new hobby, no. Her realities were merging with his, she was putting her own reigns, on him. Diet, walks, speaking privilege, and so on. She could always justify it in comparison to the other, more sinister, influences he had. Some of them were very real and he just couldn't know like she could. She knew some of it was real and some of it was manufactured. She could corroborate his experience. This invested her, as a value to him.

He began to rely on her at times. She became a load bearing staple. He called for her silently sometimes, and she would come. She engaged him intimately sometimes. She had appetites and couldn't resist. The more time she spent with him, the more control she needed. She had to exercise her will. Whenever she wanted him, she could have him, and she'd earned that.

She could leave a trail of breadcrumbs for him to find answers to his vision quest and in turn, he could be her past time. His world provided a luxury experience for her, it edified her position and status in new creative ways, while her regular life was becoming an edifice. His world was the future in a lot of ways, and in some ways, it connected, spiritually, with the past. It was an enigma, a phenomenon, and she could corroborate the crime it was for him to live with it sometimes. The persecution he felt. This almost romanticized itself. She felt the gas lighting he felt, because, like him, she could see that world he knew existed, but was told didn't.

In his life, most of the rest of the world was positioned against him and she could be a support. It was a cause, among other things. She wanted to show the world too. So, when he went off his medicine, out of his own necessity, she seized the rare opportunity to start her campaign.

She enlisted fellow celebrities, showing them the water was warm and they jumped in. She spritely played along with them in his visions and acted on fantasy en masse. The problem, though, was as enticing as the premise. She saw the promise, but had to create a bridge, between worlds, to realize it. This was the meaning it lacked. It was a logic problem that could be solved, for an ardent problem solver, that meant enticing trials and troubleshooting.

It kept getting realer. The means to an end weren't clear, but not the entire point, it was a function of living in the moment. It had a quality that relied on a dependence of belief. It was like a waveform that could collapse. The collapse was ominous, but only looming. It was a form of suspended disbelief, but in the inverse. It could be picked apart and may already have been studied. It may be the premise for rationalizing augmented and virtual realities. The premise was presumptive in value, but also self-derivative. It was like a snare. In some ways it was like America itself. Alluring and enticing but also encapsulating and entrapping. It had the elements of Vegas. "What happens here, stays here." In that way it was a free zone. A place where you could do things you couldn't normally do. That was partially the reasoning against bridging the divide, and another was rampant capitalism.

Capitalism could take a good idea and ruin it. But it may be happening anyway. This had the effect of a sale. A limited time offer. A limited time world. It also had some evidence of danger. He, Chris, had fallen victim to it once before. Fae thought she could handle the dualism she needed to personify her part in the safety of surveillance opposition to Chris and the occasional alternate, of support. She had a line to walk, but it kept her invigorated.

The implications of a whole new world were staggering. It didn't seem like something you could market easily.

Fae participated in the government sanctioned surveillance conditioning process, almost as an owner. If she wanted him infused with the bad boy element, she could send him to jail, and she did. Beyond that, the most of the dynamic was trust building exercises based on risk for intimate reward. She could see dangers he couldn't, and used that to create suspense. Once caught and in jail, she had a strict rule; we can be intimate for dinner, or you can eat, not both. Of course he couldn't resist.

The intimacy was in risky situations, keeping it spicy. Gas station bathrooms, behind convenience stores, in a bus station, on the grass outside. when it wasn't with her, it was arranged. Some of them were fellow celebrities and some of them were just people he met or knew.

Intimacy wasn't the only context for risk/reward arrangements. She also encouraged him to do things like stand in the way of people or spend his last dollar. In each situation, she'd often connect a reward for the risk, presumptively to build trust for riskier things. If she told him to go into Starbucks with no money and wait in line, a person would offer to pay for his drink. If she encouraged him to pay only a portion of an item at a gas station, the attendant would pay the rest. She had him in these scenarios countlessly, seemingly to build rapport, and it worked. So they grew closer.

She could maintain her participation as long as she engaged in the surveillance conditioning, with the rest of a host of characters. She was like a double agent, which added to the spice. It felt like a two-person revolution sometimes. Some people enact fantasies, or role play, for spice. Chris and Fae had agency that way. All this amounted to attachment, and after all this time had passed, she's lingered in Chris's corner, in the ether, watching.

Christopher J. Martindale

STREAM OF CITIZEN

Chapter 1 67
Chapter 2 71
Chapter 3 75
Chapter 4 80
Chapter 5 85
Chapter 6 90

Chapter 1

This may come as no surprise to you, but I'm crazy and that's lead to unconventional truth. It seems my lens portends a view, like I said, of someone of unconventional means to virtue. This is told because life had folds and creases for me and those a like, that border on dimensions that may strike as odd and God maketh it contentious in a duality of existence, the how and why to the way extendeth the perception suspendin' the belief, until it becomes settled beneath the folds and creases of the brain, of a man, me, insane.

There seems to be an overlayed plane where it's possible to live in two worlds the same, as it would be to have a hand in two games of chance, but there's a command some have to this game of poker and one hand between two games plays only to a hand of all jokers, even then it would be more explicable in seeming that it's more difficult, more complex and yet still, higher staked to redeeming. I tell you in prose because it's not all in the know that makes up understanding another's life. It's an extension of self to reach out to grasp what might be a paradoxical dimension of hell. This might be an older stemming from which we've read books from the shelf that speak of the flowers.

Maybe my life harkens, by it's make up, to a time where power shake-ups found crazy men to be heard for the sake of novelty.

My experience is yet unwritten, though that's only partially true, I've been withholding. The pop and appeal made me stop and turn on heel. I've had a lot to draw from and that's for sure, but my recall has been obscure. There seems to be a price to bring it back to mind, like a pay per view library. I've mentioned that currency can be attention, time, very similarly and that's meaning direct from syntax and that leads to an origin in it's making.

Like conviction leads to a sentence, there's a dimensionality to language that you can pivot from. I was lead to break the law by hallucination, so in context, I served a sentence in 1st person for a second degree offense. I was a patsy by phrase but the true culprit is only culpable in phase to me. Essentially, following to the serving. She, a female apparition, seemed to be chiefly responsible for my contrition at times. The divide between me and her something that hides in plain sight as me in their eyes.

I'm indivisible from her, I wonder if that word ever meant as much as now. Independence and freedom, both seem to veil and stand before the machinations behind the stage of politics. There seem to be a lot of things unexplained as they aren't easily spoken for. This may be why the discussions often prefer degrees, people with them and who can relate and there's a kind of Greek to the terms, a brotherhood in privilege. A status that, in herd, protects against what law is bent to deem frivolous. This is just to lay a foundation, I can't believe there'd be loads of anticipation for my story.

This prose serves as abbreviation where allegory may also serve, but I've not got the drive for. I feel and this may be received well, that the layers should be minimal on something liminal to a new view, especially one that's due to bear fruit or be doomed to be eschew. This burden of proof lies on the teller of story, not on bank letters or notes, though folks, if I could, I might exchange for those and what this means is what I have to venture forth or from in between, unearth a sum, for mining my business is like becoming prospector, the gold isn't unmeasured it's simply one bettered by counter funds. In this way, I pray you see my written word and trade bills, the same idea thrills with so many saddled from ills we couldn't possibly rationalize as paid time off, and that's it's own dry trial. Be it notes or bills, letters or sentences, I hope to convey or translate, meaning for some compensate. I do kind of ramble but that's a nature, I'm human, I hope you follow anyway.

I've decided to make this prose for effect, the ideas therein are secondary, I mean to brighten eyes and lift spirits and if I don't, I won't hear it. I've got a good defense and with a little pretense, I've got a mind to write my life how I like and this is it. Some start with a frame but I said to hell with it, I can captivate with cavitation of my brain and use language to pivot. This is stream like a spigot, I wish to alleviate brain wash with the alternative brain rinse. I hope to shower readers with lit and remit to a limit of which I might hide if I found it. I don't see a need to over organize this, I feel readership would be contented with rhymes in essence. Meaning provided or at least aspired to, in the margins or in the middle of phrase I hope to ease malaise which seems to inflict those of us with big brains. You have me captive in a way, all yours in tenses because of what I portray on paper, or even screens, I'm not sure where this will end up.

Some have been curious to my time while homeless, I can say confidently, it was a series of moments. They strung together like popcorn on a tree. There were many facets of the experience that impressioned me. At times it was strange, I was provided and deranged. My sponsor, a star, who guided for change, or so it seemed. There way a duality, at times, one that an influence seemed to derive. The power to influence turned to manipulation, where the threshold to that action wasn't difficult for the imagination. In my case, I was the subject of the whims of an inculpable entity. If you see what I'm saying, the potential was plenty. Though, in contrast, the afforded experience was often positive, I don't know to which nature It played more of, but It was electric.

From observation I was defective but, in my mind, there was an advancing directive that moved me. I could be moody to the untrained eye, but if you could see, there was felicity floating nearby. It seems coincidence, that a fae would be a name-sake, and Tina would be slang for a kind of yay. She'd act like my fairy godmother, this was strange, but one thing played on another. There seemed some directing to my visage, telepathy also catered to a sort of message. Some truth but muddled with artifice, I was thirsty for meaning and the Kool-Aid had a current. Like a currant to a date, or a date to a fig, I was a little lost in parts but bared no burden did they, when it came to fed wit. Strange to bare witness to such a collection of scenes, if it was for me only it would justify my ego indeed. Since these scenes, I've come to a theory, that it wasn't just me and that would make it an open screening. Like a drive in, and to that point I was sheltered by a car for some of it, and that mattered like gas did.

Chapter 2

I found myself in all kinds of situations, that easily played two ways, as a subject of the system and an actor in a play. I feel like there was plenty to draw from. The experience wasn't all a problem. Strangely, it jailed me still and that was not me but my ills, uncanny how that turned from thrills to cold chills. I seemed afforded and maybe that was ascribed as it seemed like I would die and that's when villains reveal their storyline. It's strange to characterize what actors can't be verified or explained in scenes. It seems to lend to a double life.

Also strange is the intersections with reality. I incurred a tattoo in bruising that spelled that out for me. Nothing was as veritable as that was to me. It made me think, how much of this bears pertinence on reality. Where do these things intersect? I'm not quite sure, and that's to my detriment. "The sky was falling" was an accurate premise in semblance. It was a theme in several shade variations and I can contest to this. There were some signals that seemed to justify this. The thickness of drinks in example, with no explicance. There was also a change in tobacco, that revelation, though, could be contested although real to me, like much else.

I seemed enlisted at times to surveille and that came with strange privilege, in essence I shepherded cars and minded photographic evidence. I mostly took pictures of license plates in strange meeting places of cars. A lot of the war games were sparse in gun play, though it occasionally rung out and as a token of fate I remained at a distance from the forays. The majority of the experience spoke to a frame of mind, you might say, where the premise for alternative realities was just an overlay. Experience determined this some, but mostly it was a game to be won. Nothing punctuated the experience quite like sex and that made me quite performative. It's hard to address, like it was the chicken or the egg. The dimensionality of it makes it hard to deduce but that seems to get me close to the truth. It was a field day and I was quite compelled to keep chasing the star. She was my orientation after all. Strangely analogous, like so many things. It kind of paints a picture of a director and moving frames. The aims were kind of illusive and the attention didn't quite seem justified. A premise for stars and military interacting with one guy mainly would set precedent.

It may have been that even one action, specifically terrorism, might have justified the entire exhibition. It did seem that there was a lot in play for powerful people but also some powerful play in a way that was meta legal.

A lot of this is in me as state dependent memory, since I remember that may mean that I'm still a little crazy and I am, but I function well enough to merit my dose, what comes close to treatment is the love I get from a ghost. A ghost is easier to talk about, though I'm not haunted as much as I'm run about. Coincidentally. I've lost some executive function, which makes me easier to lead despite my gumption.

What is today is what was wrought of my medicine free days, I wonder still if I could still relate 3 years from today, but as a craze is, it was short lived, although that maybe that it's locked up in my short circuits. I never really felt alone, and I'm thankful for that. Despite it feeling like a fad, I still wish I could go back. I wish I'd had some more autonomy and still do. It's not something that washes off of you in just a few cycles. I'm psycho, but treated generally.

I'm back in a position where I'm mentally stable, that puts my experience in a new vein as fable. That may not quite be the definition, but I defy definitions to make my own. I also try to stay in scope of understanding, life is demanding of course, I try to relate it compensated for my mental, by incrementally assailing my dissonant noise.

There are a lot of things that can be analogous to the human condition. We made things after all, and anything of self is an extension to something else. An ex once said I needed to find myself when my mind lost it's health and I've thought about it ever since. Anything ever was as it ever is just an extension of this. We are what we see to some degree as much as it touches us. We exist simultaneously, but can never be someone else, unless it's memory of it we lost. I might be several people at once by an extension of the collective conscious. I'd say as much, but I have a sense of self and that divides us. Not that we should be bees of a hive, simply that what connects us is more than being alive and that may extend to after death but that's conjecture and nothing less.

While homeless in this city, I'd done some things one might pity. I ate what I could find when I had no currency. It's crazy to me that my pittance of money couldn't feed me Tuesday through Monday. Some of that was a factor of guidance, the voices, the ghosts, the seeming contrivance. Tina had me digging through trash once and eating from the ground, other times she showed me love the most profound I've known. Her love was unlike anything I'd every felt, the sex was enough to melt my heart, her shelter, an offer to never part. In this way, we married each other dozens of times and she still hasn't parted my side. I wonder how real she really is.

The feelings exist and that's all it is for some, confessions of love continue to show up in actions from the abyss. There seems to be an extra dimension to life, it maybe why people write about things beyond average sight. I wonder the place of crazy people in history, though what I know of is their modern plight. Torturous methods were the old ways, I guess I can't complain, my heads not in a vice and they haven't cut my brain.

There's a contention within me explaining human beings behavior in enacting tragedies. My sense of right and wrong may be a little askew, admittedly, though that much is also true of human tendencies. How unnatural are somethings and how much can we agree on sovereignty? Or police brutality. I could argue both sides of some of these things and come to a state of peace, but not tranquility. I feel like I should be ready for anything, I'm not, but I'm also not drowning in make believe. I'm trying to sort through what I've got, what I've been through and define how much is and is not crazy and from that, how much is worth saying. I've been through so much, but some was time wasting. I may think some of it is garbage and some may value it. It's all kind of speculative and tenuous, to be about it. That said, there's been some curiosity and some of that really is merited.

I've had a lot of celebrity exchanges and to note, with some of them, I borrowed their voice. It was really cool and kind of arousing, at times I felt like the jail radio, constantly espousing. I had a feed of sorts telepathically, and my voice really changed, it was one of the hardest things no one asked me to explain. There were scenarios too that seemed to be tests, tests that were tailored, maybe for the best. Nuclear weapons, radiation and radon. It seemed like a test to be a president, though I don't know, as a peon. Time travel too, a strange thing to demonstrate. Unless they knew it was sealed, my fate, or at least I couldn't release that on anything that wasn't already paper mache'.

Chapter 3

There was a contingent time machine at one point made to be manually started by the whole of an NBA team. It was strange, how they'd just take that duty not to mention how hard that would be to engineer but like the Nazi symbol was derived, the design was based on something from an earlier time, a windmill. This spoke to undertones of military or secret history. This could be the stuff of Jim Mars, who wrote explicitly about what he called the "Fourth Reich" I'd read the book but it seemed fantasy, but some parts seemed true and that's were there's similarity.

The best stories bury the truth in convincing lies, making liars out of the tellers. It's as effective as a narrative making can be. There aren't that many narratives they need to discredit someone's account. Discounts sound good until they apply to your credit, this in a market that maybe perfected. I believe there's a hand in it, but that's me and my life. I think the richest truth is deciphered from the lies. Lies, like lye, can be used to clean up, ties too, on the fringe, can be tied up. There are many ways the powerful suspend themselves above us. I think we should dismantle, but that depends on if you think they've committed crimes against us. I think they have, though I'm conflicted. I feel a hard won life is well lived in, but maybe I've strayed a bit.

I meant to tell you more of my homelessness but talked about politics. Strangely, my psychosis unveiled a channel to them such that thusly I could suggest that they ingest drugs. I thought that might tantalize them and they might refocus. I personally, think the drug schedule's bogus. I believe in rat park. The idea that we don't use unless there's no us. I think that's of use to challenge that quo status. So, in my hallucination, they took to the suggestion I thought "oh what power, the most powerful profession". Government. The ability to use drugs without consequence. The feat itself would come at some expense, obviously getting narcs to do drugs is kind of tense.

Tina had her part too, in the way sex is a tool. Tina had wrapped up Boehner like thread on a spool, she had his ear, in case of a word. She'd use this privilege when he acted a turd. In the contrivance of visions he was extended family, like Tina. This goes as far to say there was a web and a channel for ideas. I was tasked as the president many times, essentially because there was always a party and they weren't invited. This is also to say that it was a hard ass job, and everyone just passed the buck. The most responsible people just couldn't take the f***.

It seemed like a headache to be the leader. So whomever got the risk meter into the black could always comeback to the hot seater. It was crazy how I got pushed over 80 where the speed limiter had to be obeyed b, I was tasked as supreme being a lot like atlas, I was made champion and got the ball for a pass rush. I couldn't get it off fast enough, I was supposed to believe that a host of machines, made my relief possible which is not unlike the stories of the turtle on the fox hill, I didn't seek the hospital when by noggin was full tilt, I just kept getting up where miss b cups leadership wouldn't fail.

It was a constant to be trailing behind her, tethered to a helicopter she hovered above me. In three years of this I went from skinny to chunky and back again willed 'cause she loved me. Though this followed at times it seemed a promise kept by pressure which I'd alleviate like a splinter if I wasn't dependent and had a penchant for depression. At one point Aesop rock voiced his impression of the situation, quizzically he said I'd fall 40 stories, I think what he meant was that at the heights she took me, the tried and true means would be her dropping me like some stolen jewelry, after all it was an affair, even if it was in the ethers, he'd maybe even figured it'd be ill fated and I'd never meet her.

I'm strained to admit it but that opinion's legitimate, unlike the relationship even marriage is culprit to ever getting with. A lot of this vision quest is about suspending a guess that would easily be correct but would leave me bereft and no matter the bitter truth, the converse was also true in how she stayed with and made the follow through. I milked at her breast on her time and won tests I think, I got no prizes or surprise drinks. I did, though, suffer shame and embarrassment at times and didn't know why but could look to the times, likely an edition, but something I didn't spy, which is crazy too, knowing something can spread wide and be aimed at you.

It was maybe a taste of a case of comisery, wanting to feel sympatico by making another live their history, I don't know. You'd think there'd be more nonsense because the leading theory is hallucinations are dreams in waking, excuse me, but I've never been stabbed by a dreamling. In jail, a vision made a picture in bruising on me, such precision and meticulosity, pleading to acknowledge the humanity, much like a cave painting leaving a record of life much like trying to send a message through time and that's wine.

In that way, I tasted the fruit of other's labor. I'd be put in place to make the case for a savior, but that of God, my heroine made clear, that the CIA is God, so maybe God isn't really here. That's a flavor of atheism that pairs with depression I'd rather keep my reservations knowing I can't replace them with a void and that would haunt me and any choice.

I will say, for an atheist, she was still romantic and it filled the same space sparing semantics. At one point I called her my God, which almost seemed heresy but, all I'd seen made that true transparently. I don't know her preference, it seemed relevant that it might've been community service, that was presumed at the surprise Mark Wahlberg in my living room.

It's strange to be famed by celebs as a secret, it's like skipping all the velvet ropes and sequins. I wonder if it was something I'd done, but don't know. It seemed I'd won the option of a show but it was for the privileged, maybe I'd made messages for god. To circumvent prayers as a term seems odd. As charity it would seem sweet as candy to a celebrity and anonymity or discreetness essentially may have closed the deal but still, I feel like a third wheel. This was my own time and place, to say that was my life and my grace, I wonder why they'd show face, just to mess around and pace themselves with my chase.

A Nazi sympathizer said it, we're like dogs. Even those who man the machines and play God? Apparently generous people, I guess if you knew you had to discuss wieners and how their made, you might relate that to the shade cast from touch, man makes on the ways of other men.

You could say it's masturbation but that's not all it is. It takes a certain effectiveness to arrange occultice. In that fashion of phrase you might make the conclusion that they could be leaders or members and mayhaps. More then once they claimed their camp. Illuminati is what they said, not very ominous or inspiring of dread, kind of seemed wed to the station of God, in his absence.

The case for trials and tribulations as a mainstay pervades. It seems, no matter the height of place, that's remained. I don't think they've worked out old age, though some claim they drink blood of babes.

There was an occasion where I saw Tina drink a vile. Maybe that's ceremony or maybe the style, it's just as likely contrived as it is wild. Somethings aren't enough as they are and I imagine that could explain visitation by itself, wanting to do good to a man in poor health the same. I don't know. Maybe it was a craze popularized by it's acceptance. I've got to say though, confessions to no God, or just dismissing outright paints a picture of a person who's maybe seen some bad sights. It excites some to think there's a man keeping score, but there are a lot of poor and we could do so much more. Knowing it's just us and not justice could popularize actions of pundits. It seems though the rub is, there's limits to room on the team of politics.

Governance seems to make party definitive, though I can't base that on hallucinations, so it's stricken. Black people, it's wild there's a caucus, I don't know much of it but maybe they're their own congress. Like I said I don't know, but it's interesting and that's obvious. I wonder how they bring their own version of progress. It seems a frontline especially in law. It seems like what's due maybe just stalled. Sometimes it seems glue, keeps a hold of it all. Though, in other ways, it doesn't seem penetrable at all. The guard they keep on what works so poorly is evident of the jerks keeping their grips on their bonds and surety's.

I digress, what you came for I possess an account of my homelessness, though I've inclined to keep it to rhyme so somethings you might have to guess. I can't cover all of it neatly, it was kind of a mess. But I think I can cover most of it if you can stand my amendments.

Chapter 4

A lot of my experience was in a car. A gas powered Volkswagen, not an HHR. I got it for free, it came with some leaks, but ultimately it took me far. At one point there was a story that it was set with charges (like I was later), that had to do with largess of political impasses, it seemed blessed but eventually caressed the inclination that detonation was best. I flirted the test, using it as a token more or less for a high stakes live action game complex. I used this idea to corral with my head, transmitting thoughts to beware or be dead.

I was the bomb and the man, but also dead pan and pissing in cans. Actually bottles though it's semantics, except that they were collected by stalkers claiming Atlantis. If you know this, that's the Aryan type, trying and vying to discover my bloodline's Reich. This was a trope, that I had some beneficial gene code they could blow, the lid off, of people in lab coats. More of the trope played me as the goat, as a reluctant hero trying his best to cope.

Politicians begged that I run the ship ashore by parking the bomb at a destination to score. I'd been influenced to action before but knew that radical action is best as a message. Blowing up a mall serving the

Space Apples

richest would just be used to oppress us. The patriot act came from the likes of this and I was reminded thus just to use it. So I did and even took pictures to prove I was with it. Suspicious cars got this. I was convinced I'd been witness to some shady auspice of oppses. I imagined them running the plates and corroborating statements but I didn't only roll as a witness.

I lived out a storyline or two, they merged a bit and pervaded the view. Somethings were quite scary and that threat might've been true, but undue. I flirted with fate sizing up big apes looking to shake down. In between dates at shake town. I thought I'd heard a gunshot one time on my old block. It had to have been near one o clock at night. It might have been murder but it might just have been outta sight. A cop seemed too casual at the same time just about, didn't hear what I heard and that had me doubt. It seemed strictly symbolic, his position, alcoholic disposition no college, be an inquisition there'd be no honest talk.

One storyline summed up my life as a herald of a new era, that's plausible if the tech is there uh. In this line I was visited by a seraphim I'd rely on for truth. She established a gas feed to my telepathic stream that verified information I'd need. I had to keep a steady flow of speech going in jail, just to ward off the possible wailing. Outside, she'd serve as Tina's contact and partner for the ride.

Hannah (her name) made what was called a Nazi deal, she wagered her soul to come to my need. This made her a kind of cursed angelic. I too, at one point, grew wings but to serve degenerates and clerics I was dismembered of them. Twice. One at the chance to fly and the other simply for the prize it was to have angel blood. It served as sustenance and a source for ritual, power and rites. This was in context of the dark worshippers on my moves like white on rice.

There were times I thought I'd have to fight and times my suffrage was caught on sight, though not combined. I had to wind up the victor, with a solid defense, I wouldn't want to have to face a judge and his bench. In perilous times I used what I could find, land surveilling stakes for one, and hard rocks, I was kind of David versus goliath half cocked. I took a fire extinguisher once and used cookware to shield potential bullets, danger made me aware or the converse, either way I was scared.

Some of the adventure was shared with Tina, this brought us closer, although I should mention she was also with a poser. Travis was a reoccurring character, kind of an all American bastard. The guy had a huge d*** and had no master, he seemed to be hers like a tool, there was maybe some legalese too. At one point we drew up an agreement to preserve our cool. Sex was big in the game, we all wanted it. It was it's own game and we had fun with it. 18 celebrity sex partners if I can recall, the time was good, we had a ball. The whole thing couldn't really be explained, much less the way my brain imagined a stabbin'. If there was more truth to it I can only imagine the consequence.

Speaking of, vice president Pence occasionally had a presence, he seemed wanton to me meeting my demise. That would have been likely in the car, but my driving was sound, I could reach that bar.

Eventually the car was towed it's last time and I thought it right that they might shine a light to it. In the car I'd thought there was a cell phone signal transmission device. At one point it held or transmitted a feed from an giant roach telling of prophecy and another time increased my hand's bone density for battle.

A theme to much of the chaos was my acts of remuneration. Sometimes I had to tend or fend depending on what ends were intended. At one time, I thought I was to fight one man and another time I was tasked to cleanse him of his own sin to begin again. This man had his own demons.

I was told I was the last of the line of Moses, which secured my position in the Jewish mafia. I, at one point, walked into a luxurious club, got free beer then sneered and threatened a guy based on telepathic information. There was a lot to suggest that the cause of interplay was morbid interest in consequence, never so bold to say kill, but certainly inclined to keep me off pills as to lead me over the hill.

There was this dynamic to recreate, like plastic, my past to explain dramatic, how I got to this and that place exact. Tina recreated the moment of mind fracture and fed my mind with manufactured story. That she had always been the catalyst to my biggest brain battle list, poignantly punctuating my atlas with legend while I was becoming more outdoorsy. This seemed to tie up loose ends of my fringe, unhinged ends retold for me, or us. Actually them but, what it made was a more potent love, by suggesting that she was always there, making fate out of thin air.

The idea was, we were meant to meet once I was of age. In my childhood she made promises that way, when she had to marry Travis as a part of her campaign to fame. The deals were made as a kind of package deal, it seemed of kabala and kind of surreal. This vantage into her life made it seem even more that she was a captive to a man Reich, that is patriarchy. Not just any, but one steeped in mystery and wizardry. I couldn't see the force behind her situations but she seemed used and maybe abused in relations. Maybe it was to be implied that she had her own guidance and there was a chain link system of reliance that binded us. There seemed a few types of this. I came across some like Jehovah's witnesses, Christianity, and Judaism. Of the three, Judaism seemed to have more freedom and togetherness. I had a dim sum of all three but was specifically run through a process of initiation for Judaism.

They arranged a lot of sexual relations and included me in celebrations. Sigourney weaver seemed to be a matriarch, that level of intrigue really made a spark when we got it on. A lot of the experience was of a rolling harem, when I was the bachelor made. The sex was incredible and everyday. There was this need to sort my playmates like f***, marry, kill almost. I wanted to maintain the reigns on the sex parade by giving each one a place. Passing me around to multiple celebrities seemed to make me more in with the crowd. This was hard to denounce as it served me, there were other times though where I was treated like a turkey.

Chapter 5

I had to deal with playing second fiddle to king jerky. That was Travis, he explained that he'd infiltrated the ranks of the Nazi's and their base off German church road. This had an odor though, he seemed to take to it too well. They seemed to gel and that made him dangerous, though she liked it, at times. He'd lay her pipe so hard it bent her spine. It seemed he'd had a privileged mission where I was kind of ala carte and half baked serving a vision. There was this strange history they all neatly wove through the scenes. One of prophecy based on baby birth d*** size fresh from the infirmary.

The tale was entrancing, Tina had chosen a mate for the future as it was to make a ritual satisfied. She had to hide her secret marriage to Travis to maintain the limelight. Relations with the kabala seemed to seal this tight. Tina had this idea that hierarchy in men was d*** size and that was kind of hard to get her to stray from. She'd also maybe had the most experience of them all so it was hard to take it from her. It was like earned.

During the sexcapades, there was some irregular behavior, but it seemed coerced. Tina's position like I said, seemed forced. She was trafficked by cops in a box and what made matters worse, is they'd take turns f***ing her, which kind of rehearsed her sexual urges. She seemed to be a nymphomaniac so abuse was murky to some, but I could see how that was a form of statutory r**e. I'm not sure that term works that way but that's close. It would be the biggest case in history if it ever became one.

It seemed that celebrities lived in a different dimension and that maybe their lives and histories were rewritten to fit them in to their lives as Greek gods. The way they lived to be believed in. In that case, Tina had been doing me the same. Maybe to join them in the other dimension. The powers that made that possible seemed supreme and that made it possible for dreams to come true, if they manipulated you. It could be one of two things, Tina, acting as agent of the entertainment dimension, was processing me for the same fate, or she was trying to make me understand her place in all of it. Obviously in the face of supreme power, some things are hard to explain. In the event that that becomes necessary, it could become clues and puzzles, which could be mistaken.

She seemed to call to me from her dimension through store radios and even people sometimes. It was magical how she would push me to do or be something some place and I'd be gifted by a stranger. She seemed to have this advanced knowledge. She seemed to serenade me through the radio at gas stations and different retail outlets. It was so beautiful, different stories were woven through and around this thread. It was the one constant, other things came and went.

Nazi deals were something we had to make to get favorable sentences and progress and maybe even to continue the whole process of sexcapades. Maybe some of them were made to extend our interplay. Maybe even the forced sex, or r**e, that she endured to pay for the experience I played in. This would be romantic and not out of the question. One Nazi deal was this way and put on tape by the Nazi I knew by name.

Potentially, they were the masters and they guarded the dimensionality. It sure seemed like power supreme and every Nazi deal seemed sacrifice. The whole time it seemed she had longed to be by my side but her situation and dimension wouldn't abide. She had begged to see me in California, when I became homeless, she implied too that she couldn't because she had used me as a token for sacrifice to enrich herself as a part of the housing crisis.

That moment in history was a precipice and great divide of richness. It put people in either the rich or poor camp. There were many benefits and she could see that as her ticket to happiness, but as the economy collapsed and my brain fractured from the sacrifice she'd incurred a price to us reuniting. This was apart of a longer game she had to bring down the money that she could share with me, if she could ever make that happen. She'd watched over me in her boredom and romanticized the idea of me. This was as much a need for her to have something to pine for as it was for me to find in lore.

She demonstrated the black magic act that fractured my brain while at a meeting arrangement she couldn't sustain. We were like reactive to each other and when we got near we became unstable as the reality would collapse and fall into place. It would bring back all the memories of her failures and forsake her story of being self made. It was sobering for her and exciting for me, she kept finding that she couldn't meet the price point or beat what she had currently, so she'd reinvest in the experience floating above me and interacting magically. She thought she could at least make it work for me and maybe that was what she meant to do.

The other way to her was just as true, she could vet me through the process by proxy and have me enter the society through it's back door. She'd enlist the help of other celebrities which mostly served as suspending the possibility, which is almost all we did. Suspended belief of tranquility and success in the different dimensionality. There was a time where it seemed she had the idea that I could use my child as the blood magic necessity to lift me into entertainment society but I'd never do it, because it meant that I'd be on the other side of the TV, watching her be all that she could be with out me, which was too hard to believe it would be better, it would be a cursed living, but I'd be married to Tina. These deals seemed for the desperate or fools and to that end maybe it served well but I wouldn't want to dwell on a bridge I'd burnt just to stay warm. I wouldn't be able to live with myself.

The deal of having a celebration of my life seemed brought on or emphasized with the death of a Jewish friend and implying that maybe he'd intended a" Jew wish" for me. The story went that he found I had a secret history in Jewish records and that I was the last of the line of Moses and that there was a false division in the family keeping me separate from Tina. There was a rumor that that alone made him a target to keep the secrets but maybe that was the injustice that caused his death.

The other friend had been dead longer and was the inspiration for a book, as a rule, the powers that be only wanted certain people in high society and that was not me. So the power of the story was what kept the intrigue. Tina admitted she had invested some magically into my efforts in writing and when she heard that I might not get it to the press she sensed foul play and left her life for a while to oversee my progress and success. She kept finding out though, that Nazi's liked us best, tragically separated and used German folk culture as a reasoning. They might have hoped I would Rumpelstiltskin my daughter or sign up for a resentment clause from the unfairness. This was a emotional protection service offered in their ranks. It could turn depression and resentment into their devil abyss where it would pool and be directed when they needed it best.

It made men as hard as iron and also their heads, making them open minded less and controlled by the abuse of their affliction. Using their curse to provoke them to action, maybe that was what was happening with Tina. What did that make Travis? Maybe it was a dual destiny where if Travis ruled, it was a Reich and if I ever reunited, it would be a more sovereign union. Either way it would be quite a fight. We rivaled each other but Tina kept it kosher between us. She admittedly, liked him like a drug but pined for me, though I felt like a mug.

Chapter 6

At one point she said I won, by a hair, it didn't serve me well but I took it like I took her care. Travis was more the affair and could handle the spotlight if it came to that. I might've been scapegoated to save that, so there was a duality. She'd long for me but got her kicks via a travesty, as she seemed to nickname him. Sometimes she'd seem to turn on him or me and that unsureness played to her being influenced some. Though she wasn't dumb, she seemed to have her own ways sometimes and unseen strings.

So, I mentioned Travis and the story they were weaving through my fringes. They were reinventing my history and that's where there were hinges and maybe a door to the other dimension, though that could've been intended analogy as their lives were in extremes to me the way they needed and nearly instantly achieved, the opportunities and privilege wouldn't make sense to me, or so it would seem. The reinvented history was mesmerizing.

Supposedly Tina was like a 7th cousin essentially but played a fairy godmother. Fae was another way of that quality; fairy. She also blessed me like that position would suggest. She also seemed to test men and their patience, by the time she'd witnessed my newborn body and Travis's, she'd already established herself as a minx. My mom's father was a scientist and her hypothesis of hierarchy in men being penis bothered him countless. My dad's dad rivaled him, though he was more classic. Between them, it wasn't clear either was more blessed by their appendage, it did seem though it lent to a bent demeanor, where one my might be a willow versus a hickory tree. Tina would play the card for her own interests and the magnetism of her sexing manifested that ending. Grandfather 1 might've been able to make the argument, but honor left it up to men to make amends with it.

There was a remuneration in consideration of birth privilege. This made a soft rivalry, as we were family, the bitter truth, that it played apart in a living infamy of Travis's deal, made it come under more scrutiny still. Grandfather 1 had ties to science and grandfather 2 had ties to the military. Grandfather 1 decided, in hubris perhaps, to challenge the hypothesis Tina presented.

The day of conception was dark and stormy and my dad was horny. They'd seemed to meet like some holiday or something unimportant. My dad had the mind to incur grandfather 1's test by using a kabala sort of magic that the matriarchs of the family had prepared (including Tina) to see their vision through. They all argued a while but tenseness became sexual and sex could be addressed via spirit machine and that's where grandfather 1 excelled. The project itself had been paid by the budget of defense, so grandfather 2 had that presence in it. Grandfather 1 had the line of Moses inseminate a member of the occultist and rich side (a 2nd degree aunt) to make an age difference but also dimensions different to see if that would be a consequence, though it was merited as that would bring my seed to fruition and make competition great, he'd be son and cousin the same.

The rivalry mirrored the grandfather's rivalry and seemed to ripple through government science, ministry, and military. Kind of obscurely, my half brother was included but hypothetically, being that he had less stake in the rivalry, but typified to be a wild card. This would make providence heavenly occasionally as it would tip the scales in my favor, if i ever needed to prove superiority, but his juxtaposition to me was enthralling. If we ever wanted to claim number one we'd each have our arguments. Travis was picked by his birth d*** difference to me. His biggest and my relationship being forgiveness in advance (for his inseminance) as they'd planned on. It obviously could warrant recompense but they'd drawn up some legality proactively, they didn't explain it but it seemed to serve their interest, maybe mainly in what they'd made investments in.

Travis's mom (my 2nd degree aunt) seemed to require the rights to life Travis acquired through her as he was apart of a test and reinforced best by Tina and that left him to her behest in a way. What made things advantageous, was the meeting between me and Travis, it would potentially render him lifeless or some sort, what they knew, was that it required some spirit processes and spirit machinists to facilitate this. Currently, we haven't met again since 7th grade, when my grandfather of science died.

There were a lot of dynamics between us, he seemed to exhibit prowess where I struggled. Most of our interactions were his benevolence to me in providence as the "big d***" he was but then demonstrating the win. Seeing as he could, it seemed inspiration romantic at times with Tina, but his largess and bad judgement made him every over privileged jerk she'd ever met, though she didn't self detest. She seemingly had no regrets, just wanted something less demanding, and I was there, after all the tests, still standing.

Travis had an equally hard time as I, because we both suffered with bipolar which meant something couldn't be good enough sometimes and we might take our own lives, though it seemed, at least on my side, that their was some reverie.

This, in summation, is the entirety of the story in prose, for details, stick your nose in my previous works. Enjoy.

SPECULATION OF CRAZY IDEAS

Chapter 1: Messiah 97

Chapter 2: Narcissism, History and Rivalry. 101

Chapter 3: Anarchist Insights 103

Chapter 4: Parallels in Propaganda 106

Chapter 5: Propaganda and Influence 109

Chapter 6: The Success of Propaganda. 110

Chapter 7: The Narrative of Hallucinations. 113

Chapter 8: Rubbing Elbows 115

Chapter 9: Diversity of Experience 118

Chapter 10: Stand Alone Blurbs 119

Chapter 1

MESSIAH

Hello mysterious reader. You may be curious about the contents of this essay. This is an essay, by a madman, selling speculation of the role and importance of mental illness in society. In this essay, I will draw and posit ideas based on confluences of history and modern time. These ideas will offer a lens at the possibility that what you believe about mental illness, may not be all it seems. Potentially, this book will challenge you to think about unlikely circumstances of mental illness and its place in human nature, ignoring for a moment, the predication of society.

My name is Chris and I suffer from mental illness. I've spent a lot of time caught in the throes of it. I've said before that it's a wealth of experience, in suffering, as well as mirth. The connections to make it interesting for the more normative people I interact with have been challenging, but worth while. I want to start with a familiar topic, Christianity. Christianity centers it's focus on a man named Christ, who was "the Messiah" of their time. Since his rise to fame, there have been others that could be viewed as messiah's. Mohammad, most notably, and maybe less notably, the Buddha. These three religions, Christianity, Islam, and Buddhism; comprise most of the world's spirituality besides, perhaps in addition, Hinduism. Some people have drawn some conclusions of overlap at the chance of uniting religions or the people in them. I know of one man, who has tried to do that with his book aiming to unite based on similar heritage of the biblical; Abraham. The author is potentially neurodivergent, but also successful. There are a lot of different experiences of mental illness and, I think some, simply are more functional and integrative.

As of modern day, bipolar and its variants, as well as schizophrenia, make up about 5% of the population. That's significant, as significant as the alcohol content of beer. In my experience, hallucinations and delusions can feel like entertainment of ideas, which is what I'm doing now. There are a lot of studies probing mental illness, but I feel like it would be better served from the perspective of the sufferer. I say this as it's a popular phrase about the illness; sufferer. So is illness, but as a story it reclaims the suffering as social value. Also, it challenges the status quo, as discourse. I think it does that by its nature of being different, but also in its ability to function as a looking glass.

Messiah, means messenger in Hebrew. Despite the contention of who is one or not. I believe it's a lot like rapper. You could call someone "the rapper" if they had a plurality in their community. Jesus was, and that's not very arguable (semantics). In my experience with hallucinations, especially recently, it seems there's a real potential for it being covert, or about sending, cryptic messages (messenger). We do this when we want added security, in tech, we encrypt messages to be decrypted by the receiver. The idea of cryptic messages to a mentally ill person, in a plural forum, may be that the intended receiver, is just open, like an open channel recipient. This would potentially clash with a power system based on control, or maybe the point of it; to subvert it in messages. After all, Christ subverted the government. I can attest to an urgency to my hallucinations, like they needed affirmation or validation. As someone uniquely able to receive and interpret messages, I served a spiritual purpose, but also had to navigate the experience. The interpretation, or determination of hallucinations is very important, but best in hindsight, after taking to medicine.

I had a long bout of highly influential character hallucinations while I was struggling to find a home. I was homeless for 2/3rds of the hallucinations. These hallucinations defined my experience for about 3 years. There was a dynamic to them.. They seemed to rely on a spiritual connotation, enhanced intuition and being built on each other. I still suffer some minor hallucinations, but it's more manageable now.

While I was hallucinating mostly, it felt like I was providing a service. It was like a Podcast, and/or influenced one, like intel for a mysterious audience. I wasn't always sure about the listeners, but I was positively reinforced to perform with status treats and sex. Status and sex and their interplay is speculated by an article in PubMed, to be the reinforcements for Narcissism. Narcissists also, anecdotally, play the victim for sympathy. I'm not a researcher, but potentially they are (maybe the products of abuse), but they are also overly driven (competitive). It's a disorder.

Potentially the organizational structure of our society in America breeds this sort of maladapted behavior, because of its brutality and maybe there's a genetic component, but there are a lot of interrelated factors, no doubt. The experience of mental illness is countered, in my experience, by those with "dark psychology"(nonempaths). These people are psychopaths, sociopaths and narcissists, but we can call them nonempaths in short. Nonempaths are believed and posited by a PubMed journal, to be what comprise "the system" as it's referred to (the dominance behavioral system). The behavior model of nonempaths is also centered on a zero-sum game (according to the same article). This is explains the overly competitive nature. If you examine our society, you may notice elements of nonempaths.

Chapter 2

NONEMPATHS, HISTORY AND RIVALRY

So I've laid out a countering force in nonempaths that defines our power structure. I've also drawn similarities with Christ. I believe there is a sort of a battle for influence and some people, like me, are targeted based on potential. This is called prejudice, but may relate to classification, those two terms relate to law enforcement and intelligence agencies respectively. Sex is the ultimate reinforcement for someone and potentially a simplistic motive to behavior. Attention breeds this though. If ever you wanted to run for office or attempt to get a promotion, you'd eventually find yourself at odds with a nonempath, being proactive against competition. Potentially, despite a larger battle or war, this take the form of small hunts. Every species on earth competes for sex. Potentially it's a rivalry as old as time. Between the neurodivergent, and nonempaths.

I think this rivalry, or some that I've had, can really be all consuming, and potentially that drive is exaggerated with those types and mine. There's a common psychological discourse about the cause of our differences. Nature versus nurture and the role of epigenetics. I believe you can trace the roots of neurodivergence resistance to non-empaths in the organizing of people in human history. I think that most of the problems we have in society, modernly, are caused or influenced by problematic people. This includes antisocial personality disorder. I think, though, whether it's intentional (what I believe) or not, the disparity and false scarcity are promulgated by nonempaths in power, according to a PubMed behavior model. I also think that the best way we're served is to arm ourselves with awareness and bolster our ability to discern, or think logically, rationally, and reasonably to resolve conflicts or hurdles to coexistence. Though these are necessary, it can be a challenge with a mental illness to resolve bias, fallacy or to be objective generally.

Most of what's established socially as norms are vehemently defended by those in power (regardless of right or wrong). Some are established via case law or precedent. I think the obstacles to arming ourselves with information like that of case law though, are put into place by authority and made significantly harder by nonempaths.

I believe there's a logical argument for ethics, in rationality. I believe it promotes personal and social cohesion and can lead to status elevation. I think we need people with high ethical reasoning to take on the people who poison the well with false rhetoric. Luckily, we get to see those purveyors on the news and in other such media. So, they aren't faceless. I think what most authorities want us to do is plug themselves into the problem-solving component, I think that's 100% effective. I think the best solutions come from those with the problem and potentially, bureaucracy is a significant barrier.

Chapter 3

ANARCHIST INSIGHTS

I'm reading some anarchist literature and beginning to think about a model that would lead to targeting one man out of millions and anarchist literature talks about the system wanting total control and having an outlier like me maybe significant. Ironically there seems to be some paranoia of insurgence in surveillance capitalism.

    I think some of my hallucinations have been partly based on real things, as some of my hallucinations aimed to prove. One such anecdote to this effect was in a conversation I had with someone who stayed at the same group home I stayed at, but right after I'd stayed. I didn't want to lead the witness with any information, so I just listened to what he said, hoping I'd resonate with it. Unprovoked, he mentioned that he thought the same person I had trouble with there, "Bill" (just Bill) the "owner" of the state funded NGO offshoot group home, had some Jehovah's witness literature. I'd seen, also, that he was episcopalian strangely, but besides that, I had hallucinated that he was a leader in that cult, very strange stuff, we both agreed he power tripped a lot and was real domineering. So, some salt in the delusion.

The witness to him also said that there was too much stealing and death, and the state got involved because of that. This was likely exaggerated for effect but based on truth, none the less. One person had died and there were problems with theft in general, weapons too at one point. He said the state routinely asserted themselves in that situation. They pretty much just kept him in check, and it was worlds better than before. Assuming they had any influence at all earlier, during my stay. Potentially, the increased government attention was gotten from an email I sent the attorney general or any number of phone calls and messages I sent.

They also put cameras up at my insistence that there needed to be that kind of "sweeping change". I think the language encouraged Bill to do it. Like "sweeping" meant I'd drop any potential case with them. It's also worth noting that after all this the organization he was apart of prescribed me twice the highest dose of meds I'd ever been on (an overdose), so I was forced to go without care until I could find another facility.

There seemed to be some big changes that happened while I was homeless afterward. It seemed like I might've had some influence. Maybe, like with Bill, the calls I made to the Indianapolis bar about being nearly suffocated by a crowd of cops in the ward, pressured the city to clean up some of the force, though that seemed to pertain to Anderson and Indianapolis, around the same time in 2020, for Anderson and 2021-2023 for Indianapolis. I also, while in jail, noticed a better jail, for one, and a lot more programs posted to their walls in the city county building. This may just be me looking for meaning, but significant none the less. There were also a lot of positive programs presented on the jail house tv. Pretty hopeful. I believe any one person has more effect than they realize.

I'm reading anarchist literature and there's some very insightful work done by Jacques Ellul in his book simply titled" propaganda" he states that what propaganda is (in America), is an attempt at influencing and converting people, molding them, shaping them, and moving them. He presents this idea that it's not a science as much as a technique, which seems to imply a hand in it. He says, what it does, and does well, is reach a mass and an individual simultaneously. This is to say, addresses them at the same time.

Personally, I think advertising is a guise for propaganda. I think it's a trojan horse used to manufacture consent to gather personal data from the population. Advertisements on Facebook can be pretty personal, in my experience, I get a significant number of ads that seem to be based on bad data, but potentially aren't. Potentially, and this is sort of pastiche, they use data heard from conversations and attempt to connect dots that may not be there. It may be Marketing AI and/or someone who makes a classic mistake in deriving causation from correlation. What I think is strange is we have these companies invading our private lives for advertising and we have a potentially motivated domestic intelligence entity(s) that may use the info. What I've read elsewhere on the internet, is that the government has private data collectors that it pays for its data collection. This is potentially the company's that we use for social media. I found one report to say that it makes up something like 15% of the employment of such enterprise but comprises nearly 50% of the budget for it. That's a pretty generous paycheck to business, if true.

Chapter 4

PARALLELS IN PROPAGANDA

Jacques Ellul moves the point further by suggesting that propaganda aims to dissolve the resolve of its listener to make them more susceptible to a message(s). At message, you could see potential headbutting with a "messiah". Besides the point Jacques mentions, what he calls, "lonely in the crowd" which is significant, I see a lot of lonely person posts modernly. He also mentions that the propagandist makes no distinction between the individual and the group, but also suggests that it attributes a group to them for efficiency.

This has me thinking, the most effective way to dissolve resolve and make someone suggestable is evident in the study of psychology as positive reinforcement. This applies to behavior, wanted behavior specifically, theoretically, the best way to reinforce behavior is with both (constant) negative reinforcement and then (instances of) positive reinforcement (if you randomize the positive reinforcement, you reinforce it further), this is exemplified with good cop bad cop. Or a prevailingly lonely atmosphere paired with occasional hope. Media has many applications for this but notably in television and movies. Modernly, there is a glut of such examples that render people docile and encourage domestic behavior, priming them for messages and potentially unconscious ones. Advertisements are often that way.

The insight to these conditioning effects can be made with self awareness and self inventory. Rationalizing emotions renders them. I used to do this in my leisure time as an adolescent and I think it helped shape who I am today. I call it homework. Spending time with myself and how I feel to explore it. This mainly applied to social interaction but, potentially ads, media or people too. I think this is paramount to sovereignty.

Applying ethics and adhering to them also bolsters resolve. By withstanding negative behaviors to your threshold (tolerance) you passively garner goodwill. There is a phrase of wisdom I can think of that says, "steel sharpens steel,". It's important to stay sharp. Sharpening steel with steel also manifests magnetism. It's better to be a warrior in a garden, than a gardener in a war.

What I mean to say generally, is that tolerance is best practice in social contexts, but boundaries guides this and then, finally rational, reasonable, discernment informs an answer to a stimulus. We all have karma, or effects, we don't always see it, but it could be just out of sight.

More to the point of the person as subject and the group as a target, Jacques Ellul writes that when resistance has quelled, that propaganda has achieved its means. This has been my problem and an effect I've noticed on myself in a way. I've had a more direct contact with a "shadow hand" per sé, and this speaks to my experience with hallucinations as cryptic and potentially confidential messages, but also interactions as tactile hallucinations. They're a response to oppression. Early in this recent streak of hallucinations I began to suspect that I was getting hallucinated effects from people I knew or met and I began to call them out as I had the chance and they were revealed in the hallucination! It was biblical almost, like a revelation.

Chapter 5

PROPAGANDA AND INFLUENCE

Jacques continues to say that propaganda seeks to influence the belief in myth. Movies are modern myths and media reinforces myths too.

Chapter 6

THE SUCCESS OF PROPAGANDA

Jacques continues with a diatribe about covert propaganda versus overt propaganda. Overt, or white, propaganda serves as a mask for covert, or black, propaganda, where it creates an implicit reasoning, where it's open ended, and a duality of near comparison. Muddling the truth this way effectively quelches dissent. I believe that this technique can be seen in news media where they kind of nick, dissenting sentiment by sewing so close to it that its difference is hard to discern, it's nearly gaslighting in that effect. Just touching on it. Being proactive and having the sense to gauge how to handle dissent or counteractive ideas really illustrates how prevalent intelligent design is in our lives. Under the guise of social media, internet cookies, mockups for advertisements or even Nielsen ratings.

There also seems to be a wash of inclusion, where if you can get different hands on it, for example, business and pay them accordingly, you kind of manufacture consent. You also can't fully point the blame at the government, when a business full of citizens also participates, it washes the karma. In my hallucinations as, a person with mental illness, I called It karmic laundering, this is when you convince others to participate in the processes of the machine, or against it and that, not only shares the culpability, but creates a network for a keen operator to play to

Jacques Ellul uses the term "mania" at one point to illustrate a social effect, like a wave. This seems to imply a correlation between people and personal mania. This may be an actual metaphysical connection in relationship to the masses, this would make mania obviously not great for a power that wants to consolidate. This points to bipolar and mania generally being a symptom of something going on with a larger group, though maybe not. But that would be reason to want to influence someone with mania, but especially, through hallucinations. I used to think my mood was tied to the economy at large for example.

I think there's some truth(s) in my hallucination experience but like I've mentioned about propaganda, there's a duality to some of it and a masking of it in terms of psychiatry. But dismissing hallucinations may also be harm reduction and not seen as gaslighting. I feel like it shares some features of propaganda or the air of propaganda where it would feel necessary to have stealth messages and sex and stabbing a tattoo in my neck to prove its validity as an experience (a hallucination left a bruise tattoo on my neck, a picture). I also had an experience two-fold of the same thing twice, a force field. I was smoking behind a strange bar and got the feeling that there was a sort of invisible wall in the alley way, I threw a quarter, and it arced but then bounced back midway through its arc! I also had this experience in jail and, while on camera, tried to show it working by running my head to the door and it stopping me. Through a lot of my experience, I relied (and was possibly suggested to be) on camera footage to kind of be proof of my condition and occasionally (but not the first time) I believed that higher ups were buying the footage. I have no proof of it, but I was very performative on camera. There was also camera footage of cops asphyxiating me at a ward, I've never seen anything come of it. Potentially there are things going on in the background I'm not aware of. After all somethings have gotten better.

    I had a hallucination that I was a "guest at the table" with Barack Obama. It was odd because I f***ed his wife, spiritually. He included himself in kind of managing me, it was strange. There was also a time where he seemed to be elevating himself to a higher power and I could check him against that. I was given a kind of strange temporary passport to secret clubs. This started early in my hallucinations and weaved truly through them. There were a couple times I made note of people across the aisle that I admired like Boehner and Rand Paul. It was odd, at the same time I often felt like the veins in my head might pop. I share a medical history of a disposition to ministrokes, which might be a part of my files. I had a habit of watering my head or, at one point, taping my neck to alleviate the pressure. There seemed to be a want to Knick me into nonexistence, one of these ways seemed to be by popping the veins in my head to have me stroke. Potentially it was conservative power play, I imagine it takes the fun out if you can do it easily (kill), but more the case that that's not best practice. I interacted with Bernie Sanders too but limitedly, I had a suggestion for him about sex insurance, I thought it would be a good idea to have it at one time, making the argument for having sex. It's strange how I was elevated but also, rubbed the fellow higher ups the wrong way, at least some of the time.

Chapter 7

THE NARRATIVE OF HALLUCINATIONS

Parts of the hallucinations are consistent with a narrative and parts of it seem to point at me hallucinating as they aren't very consistent. Potentially it was a curated experience by Space Ex, as seeing the stars isn't as immediately intriguing as f***ing them. There was a part at one point in my sexcapades, where I was getting frisky in a port-a-potty with Courtney Cox. I didn't really want to, but it wasn't really a choice. Just before that, there was some interaction with Sigourney Weaver, using some sort of tool on my brain and isolating where my problem was, it was therapeutic, but also kind of informing of my condition. I said, "there's the camera, get it". She seemed to just massage it and leave it be.

My hallucination of prominent Jews was a narrative of wisdom of elements of power. My hallucinations of African Americans were a real mix, not so much just one way. Tribal per se'. Whites were typically in the form of Nazi's skinhead and white supremacists in general. I had a lot of sex in my hallucinations (about 44 sexual partners total in 3 years). Anyway, there were also battles where I was empowered enough to take on Nazis, zealots, skinheads, and pedophiles, the most interesting were the pedophiles as they seem to portray themselves as gepettophiles, or petafiles which had different meanings, but had some truth to them. They seemed to be veiled quite well to normative peers and had unusual gifts often. Unlike Nazi's, you couldn't easily hold them to trial, they were networked so well which was kind of ominous, they cloaked easily and seemed to often be intelligent manipulators and particularly charming in the case of my hallucinations. Child porn is really dirty business and so is the internet sometimes, potentially they build cases and presumptively charge them. I haven't seen much of that, I think we have a real problem with tech literacy, even in professional fields. I addressed a question concerning their capture at one point, like how to search for child porn users without seeing the porn and I suggested filters for skin tones and time signatures for the duration of the videos. Time signatures seemed to make the most sense. It was a dirty business to even make conjecture about and quite scary. Zealots, Nazis and skinheads were too but that fight was always on the horizon not next door.

Chapter 8

RUBBING ELBOWS

I had 3 suggestions I can remember sharing with the couple of politicians in my hallucinations, 1 was, let republicans say the n word in a special meeting of congress and for just one day. Just let them get it all out and over with. Another was sex insurance, I don't remember my reasoning, besides having it, but it seemed like a good idea at the time. It would encourage sex but also pay out for things like screenings, birth control, abortions and full-term births, also, if you had a child and discover they have a disability, it would cover that too. Having a kid is kind of a gamble and I think it would make a good rebuttal against the "prolife" people. Another thing I suggested was politicians experimenting with heroin. I think we're all curious, but, with all that power, potentially that limits their experience, where it could be broadened otherwise. I thought that might get some experience on the matter of scheduling drugs and possibly getting clean needle exchanges. In my hallucinations, they had the special meeting of congress for the n word and got the grace period to try heroine. I also saw a clip of Obama seemingly strung out on a strange news edition that covered some modernizations of certain communities. It showed a lot of technology, likely being subconscious in effect. The third idea, which would be favorable to sex workers and women in general, wasn't really acknowledged. Shame.

There were times also that I may have had a seminal experience to that of comic books. I was dosed with radiation a few times, and a couple times, I was a witness to things that might not have been on the news. Once, I was dosed while trailing a firetruck while running around looking for a "leaving party" from the state, like there was an evacuation. (Which could've been a drill). Another time, I was dosed while huddled up in an abandoned car, and even another time, I was troubleshooting the vantage of my eyesight (which seemed to be shared) and no one could agree on how it looked but I , simultaneously, also voiced policy that, if it could be done, sperm regeneration should be limited to manage the population and I was used as a sample of a treated dose of radiation, for that purpose. I've seen movies of some kind or another, that have shown that high profile targets are often watched via infrared, maybe I was dosed with radiation to make me more visible on radar, I'm assuming that someone can be dosed with it at all and remain healthy, if that's the case, it would wear off and potentially the half-life would be calculable as a time frame for the surveillance. Potentially this draws analogy of stars, being high value targets by chance, with their own surveillance. I don't think it's odd that the state would want to monitor some people, especially as they have afforded themselves, or produce/are capital (to the state). This would be of interest as those surveilled would be actively independent and the state might not want a lot of that. Alternatively, it may be that someone with such activity comes under review often by the state. I've been very conservative about my information in its exposure and maybe they even prefer surveillance as a practice. It wouldn't be too strange to illicit participation from idols, but it's hard to rationalize it. Maybe surveillance is covered by defense budget spending, that could roid up the surveillance complex. Maybe they have a lot of freedoms and goodwill. Conjecture mostly.

Still another time, while I was driving around the Midwest region, I seemed to have witnessed what looked and felt like fallout. It just rolled in like clouds of smoke over the traffic into the state of Michigan. It was a crazy time, it was also on the border of Michigan and Indiana, potentially there was a story to it, but I never heard about it. The idea that a target is dosed with rads for surveillance would seem to make a positive correlation to comic book characters. Potentially, movers and shakers would have to be monitored and were extraordinary as it was but made heroes by their vision and fortuitousness. Radiation would acknowledge their power.

Chapter 9

DIVERSITY OF EXPERIENCE

I had an experience with time travel. Time sped up. I watched as my body went through motions and cars passed quickly, it was very strange. I experienced that again one time while on meth; maybe to muddle the experience. Potentially, some secrets are too good to just hide all the time. This might point to sympathy for my condition, in the ranks of power. It may also be a sign of good faith, but I know that good deeds should merit themselves and I'm better served as a skeptic. I could get lost in the positive. This is also a scrutiny of the standard we should have and holding out hope that we reach new standards. Getting away from that could affect it's achievement. Positive reinforcement is helpful, but it's like sugar and if you have standards, you potentially model the behavior. I also prefer my sugar diluted. I think that we owe it to those who could seek to advance the status quo, to doing so, and we should press that. It's complex and progress is slow, but possible, although I think it should be minded as maintenance, and good things are well maintained. That also reflects well on the maintainers.

Chapter 10

STAND ALONE BLURBS

Social Theory

I've been trying to find terms to illustrate what I see in my study of people and found one called "cult of success" and its meaning is thus: if something succeeds, then it ought to succeed; its success is proof of its inevitability, even its goodness. I see this, and potentially this prophetic thought as a fallacy. Fallacies are so important to being conscious. Potentially we just can't make the connections between why and the nearest, most rewarding connection, is prophecy. That connection may be unconscious bias, or it may be influenced. I think this is like mysticism and mysticism is like magicians, there's a way that it works that we just can't see. Potentially it's a study in bias or blindness, Maybe, also, it speaks to the shadow of the market and it's lottery like effect. It may be a dark art in application, like how some people perform tricks, tenders to the market may have tricky means, or play to our biases and fallacies. Success, like the market it's in, is mysterious but more specifically cult-like. Potentially there are purveyors. But potentially it follows more definitively, like something we can calculate, or observe. I'm trying to sort out how much of what is effectual modernly as an extension of human nature and how much is intentional. I think they're equally interesting, but first, a surface glance. Maybe people group like blood clots form around a wound. This doesn't explain much of the human element and may muddle that to hide tending to it. The analogy just serves as an observation. In my search for meaning, especially in terms of success and disparity, I wanted cult of personality to have a better definition, like the tendency for electing personalities to higher status more generally, but maybe that's just me.

As an integral side note, I've noticed, occasionally, changes in certain language presence, in its availability to be searched, and definitions of similarly dislocated words or phrases to be missing or changed. There's an interesting verbal history to our language and sometimes powerful turns of phrase are turned around. I think this is potentially intentional as a battle for language is a battle for culture. There is an example I can think of in "pick yourself up by your bootstraps" that was a worker's phrase to illustrate the lack of comprehension of management, but now management uses it. This may have been a motivation for Noam Chomsky and others to study linguistics. There are many worker folkisms that didn't seem to make it to modern language. On my search for meaning, I also noticed there wasn't a phrase for herding, as people, which could be easily called the cult of conformity. It's easily substituted for herding, but herding is not distinctly ascribed to being human. This is a kind of reductivism, and I feel reductivism is pertinent to hiding your math, or proof, and maybe disingenuous. I think, also, it has birthed a lot of phrases, like "blood is thicker than water" meaning wise. It seems to be that confident idiots make the language sometimes. Conversely, I believe the confluences of language, science and math aren't so distinct to me lately, I feel like there is a kind of math to language in the way it's been formed and what it lends to in the mind. Potentially that's a frontline of science, and potentially true of ChatGPT's successful language model. I think progress, that way, maybe just as pertinent in advancing culture as E=MC² was to physics. If we can understand it.

    I feel there's a language to math and I think the inverse may also be true. Potentially that could be a study, though I haven't seen it, (it may be linguistics). Another side note; It's also interesting that Indianapolis's football team is called "The Colts" when I believe we got the name, and the team around the 20 years after Jim Jones. Potentially we couldn't be called cults lol. Anyway, I've been told that, being a student of people is rewarding, at the least, and maybe pays off even. I've noticed things to that effect. I feel like there are a lot of dynamics that define our experience as an individual, but also as groups or demographics. I see the delineation and discernment of the conscious and unconscious, in our American lives, as paramount to empowering ourselves, it's a necessary pursuit to being conscious consumers in a market and even better yet, producers in our own fields. This drives me personally. I hope you find it interesting. Let me know if this interests you too as I may be inspired to write about these things, (I did) the choice is only if it would be a study, bluntly, or a story, flowery. Thanks for reading, Cheers. *edit* Jim Jones was late 70's and we got the team's name from Baltimore in the late 80's* still interesting.

Death and dying
5 friends of mine have died in the last 4 years. It has me thinking of the line by rage against the machine "those who died are justified, etc." I really feel like it's America that kills, I don't even mostly think it's choices. I do think, some are more insulated than others, but no one's got more than a lifetime guarantee, in that your lifetime depends on them and they aren't liable, but they've created the social landscape where people can't pay bills or feel alienated from their peers or can't

get treatment. I feel like you should be able to charge the state with second degree murder, who's to answer for their deaths? If it's no one, then it should default on the state, but more than that there are bills to pay after death, who must pay? We all know we're behind most developed countries socially, but it's not esoteric, real people die. The state has a unique right to pick up cases where a victim might not pursue charges, this doesn't seem much different, it's due diligence. I just know it will kill more, but it releases its liability. I'm worried about the potential of death I see for some people, current friends even, and I just can't believe some of the stories I hear where people struggle so hard and don't get adequate services. I don't know if anyone feels the same, but I just think we should be prudent, America doesn't post disclaimers.

Crazy notion #2
Have you ever heard of the term fishbowl? It lends itself to meaning, or at least seems that way. Meaning in this way is strange but significant. I used to work with a guy who'd say, "I get what you mean". It was real charming, I think it's worth examining how we know things. I often have to check my rationality. I have experienced knowing things without a clear source and that seems significant to me. Knowing things is kind of magical in a way, it is in this way that we infer or translate our experience and that's really satisfying. This feature of being human really drives being social. Music is especially this way and translating emotion to others effectively is what makes it an art and the artist successful. I feel like some of us with experiences, we'd like to share, feel this. I wonder though, if there is maybe a plane for knowledge. I wrote a little about the supraconsious in my book and detailed an experience I had being above the plain of thought and it was strange, it seemed to say knowledge is meaningless if it's all from somewhere else and not totally definitive of us as a person. I was experiencing this

in a time where I was listening to Matisyahu and he had a song where he detailed planar consciousness on a scale of 1 through ten. 9 was knowledge, or knowable, 6 was instinctual etc. Anyway, just thought it was interesting. Thanks for reading.

Crazy notion
Attention seems to magnify responses with added pressure to any given situation. They mention sometimes that Facebook tends to polarize. I think that extra ingredient is attention. We might not have given much credence to some if it weren't for social media. With that premise, what if, you had instead, a platform free of accountability, a 2nd class citizen as a reluctant subject and people who crave attention. What I'm giving you is a premise of my hallucinations. What I mean to imply is that the attention would polarize, not only the person, but potentially the people on the platform. This could have all kinds of unusual results. Like delusions of grandeur etc. What if also, it had an allure in its secrecy/unaccountability. What if it was like Vegas," what happens here stays here". Would it be enterprising? I find it odd too that Facebook is now Meta platforms, what if, in recognition of a dimension of human experience, someone anticipated development adjacent? A business model modeled off the schizotypal experience. Just a thought, thanks for reading

Strange notions #4
I got a craving for crack today, paired with a flashback. Nobody can prepare you for how real life gets when you're crazy and homeless. I say that like people plan on homelessness, in a way though I think some people do. I did in a way, and that came out of my mouth today. One of the reasons was instability at home and what I noticed was a kind of deficient disposition I had. I struggled a little more than average and I was aware of it. That didn't mean I wasn't smart, just a little deficient.

I'm still aware of the street and the allure of freedom. I've got diagnoses and medicine, and what I was missing recently, I'm now getting some days. Connectivity. I've got my problems and it's ok. Somedays are worth the sweat. Somedays just aren't. I have unique problems and that doesn't help my connectivity. Plenty to write about, good and bad. But it's hard to explain hallucinations that act like managers. R**e is also hard to explain in that way. I've got meaning, or I find it rather, and that's a calm candle light. Sustaining. I've been trying to justify my life to myself, or more so, waiting for it to happen to me and I get sabotaged and picked at and manipulated by my hallucinations. The call of the void is a very real experience for me, I feel drawn to misery, there seems to be a real meaning there. In misery. Romantic sometimes, tragic other times. I'm looking for a justification of life, a reason to be and I just haven't found one yet. I keep going because it's still the path of least resistance. Mystery keeps me engaged. Thanks for reading.

Strange notions #2
I feel like mental illness can be a threat. And in that lens, it would be a very effective silencer of spirituality or free speech in general. That may just be the reason for what I've been calling "the phantom saboteur" or "shadow hand". I'm surprised to think of it so easily. It serves as a warning to nonconformists, who are just people poorly served by society. This also lends easily to the system just being narcissists with common interests that converge instead of outright conspiracy. I've always imagined it like this part in a favorite book I read where there's a god game and you are challenged to influence one species to beat another with the least intervention possible. Like a good golf game. I feel like that's the name of the game with the "shadow hand" or "phantom saboteur" and there might be real stakes. It would also fit a narrative of omnipotence somewhere in our culture, somewhere, somehow, there are levers and strings that people pull to make it how it seems. That

may be why some people are so cynical too. Cynicism is just defensive idealism after all. I feel like, if I had true freedom (and I don't) I could work on the resolution of this, alas, that may be why I'm disturbed so vehemently, if you can imagine a system, that can infiltrate every aspect of your life, it would have to be maintained simply because it exists and because it exists opposing a majority (my theory) it would have to be used to float the other side of the equation. It would eventually point to slavery and exposure would demand recourse, I imagine that drives it too and maybe even the political rhetoric of people who simply want to maintain power. Be bold, but be braced, the system will defend itself.

DISSENT INTO MADNESS (POETRY)

Chapter 1 129
Chapter 2 138
Chapter 3 146
Chapter 4 153
Chapter 5 163
Chapter 6 172
Chapter 7 181
Chapter 8 189
Chapter 9 198
Chapter 10 207
Chapter 11 217
Chapter 12 226

Chapter 1

RULES FOR ART

Find your life through it.
Leave something to be desired.
Let your love go.
Let love find you.
Take your strokes broadly.
Go to the fire, not from it.
Love bravely.
Take risks.
Believe in dreams.
Believe in prophecy.
Believe in proportion.
Wager what you can afford to lose.
Be as straight and true as the arrows you shoot.
Be about what you're about.
Take aspect from those you respect.
Learn to gauge seriosity when learning from someone.

Christopher J. Martindale

Don't write anyone off.
Look to sages.
Choose questions wisely.
Be aware of the passage of time.
Look to those who have already contributed.
Let your energy lead you, not control you.
Let your only crimes be of knowledge and commit to learning.
Know this: anything can be art if you appreciate
Choose your company wisely
Living for art is committing to a fight for your life.

A SCHIZOTYPAL LOVE SONG

Squares in rows
Rows of patches
Patches of cloth
And badges of poesy

Love struck thunder f*** bag a bones homie,
Patches where the weeds won their victory,

Muffin studs button punching my kisser bluntly,
The victory simply showing the vulnerability,

Plump and juicy butt punk funk dunking bunky,
Vulnerability showing a potential,

Shit swish pith's kitsch switch hitch,
Potential laying itself bare,

Mister blisters whistling dixie up fish craw,
The bareness showcasing virility,

20,000 and one and it's up yours with a thunder gun,
Virility normally veiled for decency,

Hot and sweaty two-toned daisy's and three kinds of marmalade,
Decency vaguely echoing sexual viability anyway in shades of grey,

Think as much as you want, you can't escape it,
You were born to copulate,

Everything you do is a mating dance shy of thrashing penis,

Wake up in the posies and its p***y,
Go to bed in dong valley,
It's a wet dream away from achieving you highest purpose,
Cumming.
While hallucinating a less harsh world than the actual one outside of yourself,
Leaving you longing to meet it by doing the next best thing to cumming,
Dying
But dying is consistently double booked in the brain.
As an end, and a transition,
Of consciousness,
The allure of it, drawing out life,
Emphasizing a lurid meaning to exist at all,
And in its usherance,
There is a tandem duality,

RECONNAISSANCE

Running zigzags, and hugging facades,
Like damn this fuzz is odd.
Is that a scope on his Glock?
For me, I think,
Still running,
I don't have a piece,
Is it police just fronting?
Strange cops, covert ops,
Why me? Why are they ducking?
Followed, and scoped, I'm all prayers and hopes,
Breathless and tired, I relax, no one fired,
Seems strange, I wake up and my pockets just change,
Phone is gone, why steal it and leave my wallet?
So stealthy, felt the threat of emissaries,
Fleets even, might not take much to yeet them,
Commandeering,
Maybe sense is at least good for possible danger,
Those shadows aren't gang bangers,
I swear I'd testify I saw with my own eyes, guys pursuing,
No proving though and they're likely confident,
My nights spent eyes wide open,
Looking at followers,
Didn't make me any less vigilant to coppers,
But this seamed of war games,
Maybe spoke to some frames of hallucination,
The mode of stealth communication,
Illustrated two sides in action,
One of my rights,
The other grouped against, and hence,
My plight is less tense,

Christopher J. Martindale

But now my funds are down,
Just one more coincidence,
Impingiance consistent with discontents maligned,
Sorts doing reports and retrievals,
Not evil but opposed,
In short, reconnaissance,
Think long on it,
It's still my purport,
And it's lost on most.

MY MENTAL PUSH

Government project,
Extra judicial, extra sinful,
Hires free agents extrinsic influence in full,
Hinges, since impingiant effects on affect deemed significant,
A staff hired to take watch might only be dismissive,
Could be just me, all subversive,
Tied to a brand of sedition,
Not only coercive but made malicious,
May their cause be a multiple head mission,
To counteract my cognition,
In Latin,
Inhibit neuro ignition,
And see through the cancelation of subscriptions,
Brain diagram pentagrams triangulation,
O2 is missing, bottle necking resonance to read encephalogram,
Bit annex bits in,
Void execution control quit it, modus operandi, deny transmit.
Effective to effective directive advanced to wit,
Do not pass go.
Do not collect 200 dollars,
Passed through jail,
Maybe even passed a pundit holler.
Meanwhile NGO entity versed as enemy.
Grant project stamp boils down to indemnity,
Lone agency admission leaves reversion,
Not conversion,
But coercion out of court pled to fore inertian as remedy.
No bullwhip or bailiff,
Just cops on promenade,
Interaction subtraction,

Christopher J. Martindale

Passing legions of demagogues,
I'd perspire as possessed,
The t9 combined with allession,
Might untwine my minds compression to alay the pentagon,
Although my uptake might pump fake like it does with cannabinides,
My composure, might doze sir,
Know why I can't hide,
Being legal literate the embedded meaning in sentencing,
Allude to philosophy adjudicate, but practice is syphilitic,
The outside of the pen upstate, justice achievements, inefficient,
The empirical reality is summed a sociality,
Might fight for life but end an unheard tragedy affiliate.

AVENUES

All these avenues to pursue art become tracks.
I wish I had my own path to go after what people perceive I lack,
It's for a fashion I have to craft a locus mode of control,
Like a rocketship's gyroscope,
Without one I float,
If it wasn't for what I've wrote, I might not be able to cope.
Oh oh, if it's to be, it is up to me and so it goes,
I feel it's woke to be predisposed to outlay my innerworkings in prose,
I compose with a little composure,
My life's adventures weren't in a brochure,
I'm more akin to a schizophrenic grocer,
Whose presence reminded me you can be a beacon of energy,
In life's strifes, it's written on you, your plight,
But also, your might,
It's like an advertisement of light,
We've all got signature beams when someone brings up something,
That brings meaning or just lifts your spirits,
It's not easy to see the merits of a life with less ease.
We need more grass seed to make grassroots I perceive this, and my life is proof.
It's hard to get ahead on my own when I wonder like a man without a home, truth,
But despite blunders it's possible to get support,
I do purport, but what's here's been here and we need something new of course,
If you hold the ladder for me, I'll hold the ladder for you,
What's construed might not be water or food, but it can get us through.

Chapter 2

SYLVIA PLATH

Sometimes, I feel the void,
The calling of it,
I'd like to bake my head in an oven,
Like a true writer,
Sylvia Plath,
No half-baked ideas in her coven,
She likely had the plague, like me,
Of a mind ever restless,
Ability to subvert the kind of intrusive thoughts that coalesced,
As an outline of her life like a plot,
The macro of it seems to tell a story so distraught from the outside,
Like her death most compelling,
Might need redressed for the telling,
what wrought of a life may be significant,
Or the pith of owning a chamber pot,
Though might not wished to be defined by lack of prosperity,

She owned an oven too,
Might've had less disparity, but that's not gleaned mainly,
What seemed is she sought to cure her life as the end served the means,
They always tell you do not, don't you worry, life gets better but it's hard,
Pitted against a viciousness with a semblance of composure,
Then to be so short served at a short blurb as obit,
Compared to how it's turned out, her legacy was her final act, lived after her in infamy,
The affinity for her framed as that, but the duality of the gab saying don't do that,
But do it right, we can't always make it to night to put it to bed,
Maybe it'll be alright and it's all in my head.

Christopher J. Martindale

BASKET CASE

What's there for me remains to be seen,
Like an open casket,
Might be a wild case bombastic,
Not just basket,
Like I'm counting eggs that haven't hatched yet,
It's such a strange phrase,
What would I do with it?
I guess I could pivot like its basketball, but wasn't it peaches originally?
I think that's a good call,
When life hands you peaches make a basket,
Unless you can task it to someone else, who can hack it,
Basket weaving's boring I imagine,
Nobody does it, that's the case,
If you're a basket weaver maybe it's just your taste,
Maybe we shouldn't judge,
By its contents, even if it's eggs or waste or peaches,
We need gumption,
To assess your function, much easier to see inside by their speeches,
Just ask them a question,
This is already quite a collection of conjecture,
Maybe their mind is a defector,
Missing in action, maybe they're a collector,
Of rocks like garden variety birds,
Maybe it's for the birds,
Hence the coo coo birds eggs,
And it's nest,
I can put this to rest, a basket case making a case for baskets,
And other basket cases is a test,
And I test positive for salmonella,
But all the cracked eggs make an omelet,

Space Apples

O fella, they tell a short story,
Crack an egg to make breakfast but it's hectic when morning's eclectic,
Got my head trip and the mess is causing wet drip off the pan,
Should've cracked them not just smashed them with my hand,
What a case for baskets now!
And accounting for taste, ciao,
I've got a place to clean now.

Christopher J. Martindale

FORMALITY

This might be a formality or a consequence of fallacy,
But I'm definitely not an example of normality,
At best I'm bright and full of witty insights,
Of writing my truth,
I have a mind and I've retained my youth,
I might be spoofed, in theory, televised, I might query on my phone,
it's suspicious how their subjects are like my own,
It would be convenient to say it's conspiracy,
Another theory: it maybe they, and I,
Share a source of ingenuity no one owns,
Or maybe it's free notes, news on regular folks,
Might be a source, might make for easy jokes,
The NSA could be a friendly gab bazaar,
If you're in the upper class it might be served with caviar,
Writing for stars would have a vast supply,
Know why it's a premise,
Farming the government's pig stye,
Would be a reason for classification,
But why listen to a crazy,
When you can continue the feed your filled,
Nothing wagered, nothing won.
Though I ramble and I know I do,
But it feels true,
Call it mystery, call it magic,
Could be misery, could be tragic,
All these things share a similar aspect,
Just know, although passive,
Your apart of the action,
Whether or not it meets your satisfaction,
Might not serve you, if it's not your purview,

Though it's enlightening,
The true cost of knowledge is often frightening.

STATIC

Something's, if you're like me, feel like static,
Somethings from most peeps seem idiopathic,
The lengths people go for fashion is drastic,
When it seems like cultivating yourself might be more fantastic,
Compared to layers and layers of plastic cast out and landed on the grasses,
Disadvantaged,
Why make earth pay for your existence,
What makes that worthless should be insistent,
People go through at least some small effort to seem distinguished,
From the rest of earth,
Seems pert, but they're curt and all the evidence points to short sightedness,
Not all their fault, sure of that, but why don't they feel called?

PHANTOM GUIDES

Am I lost on pills, kind of a dangerous thought,
Though I bought in while distraught,
And pinned the idea to a thought,
I wasn't so caught up in it to escape the unpleasantries,
There were somethings, like amenities,
In the living, I forgot,
Somethings were provided,
The coin two sided,
Token vices and non-prescribed violences in insecurity,
But still abided, my phantoms guided,
Lost yet found, how do I describe it?
Maybe confided a little too much already,
My hand is steady penning this,
Maybe a loose penny, another one and that's plenty,
Two cents at the ready for a friend, and it's henny,
I shouldn't drink, I know I shouldn't drink,
But I'm letting, my mind get ahead of itself,
Yesterday I read the Mind That Found Itself,
And it's less descriptive than I thought,
More talk of nerves and shudders than hallucinations,
And it was an earlier time,
My need for an affirmative testimony is coming up double bogie,
Why is my plight so different?
Why do my open doors come off the hinges?
I need some affirmative affirmations after consternations livid,
I'm beside myself,
Can't deride myself,
If I've got someone else,
Might stealth put the bottle back on the shelf,
And go back to minding my health.

Chapter 3

ART BAPTISM

Baptized by trial and error,
Or on the frontlines of thought,
I think that's Avant Garde,
Maybe what it's not,
What's defining, maybe pushing how far society's got,
It might also be a philosophy, that drives the plot,
A picture says a thousand words,
But what of frames shot, how much does a movie say?
If you could paint it in a day?
The business of art is in its own pittedness,
Art, and artists tiff and I'm a real witness to this,
In my own differences, that's the better plight, because art's not war,
It's none the less, at least aversiveness, confronted with assertiveness,
The real work of our cultures is hot to cool like fresh from pot,
A stupid lot wouldn't know this,
But proponents know it takes some watts,

That's power as it's used, closest to raw in its form,
It does what we need it to, nothing more than what we made it for,
And what an example in metaphor, we do what we want,
Despite being easily made, we don't just do what we're made for,
And that purports a lot of philosopher's modern thought, cumulatively,
But still more of it is spoons than tv, as for consumption,
The imbalance as a premise, not a challenge to write about,
It's maybe usual, but I'm also delusional sometimes, and so I write,
Lots to pen, when, in your mind, there's a fight,
You gotta win.

Christopher J. Martindale

I'M HERE

I'm here and I'm still at it,
Like an addict to reason why malfeasance could be,
While the great machine processes me,
The dawn of AI paired with automation means I still have to prove I'm a guy,
When I'm prompted but like hi, might be a person on the other side,
Not just ChatGPT contrivances alive in tenses,
Might have to argue my life, and some coincidences,
Synchronicity becoming synchratic,
Some of what we do now's automatic,
Even systematic,
Makes for a new scope of frame for the batshit insane, how,
Or does it, get in your head like an earworm,
Gotta listen to it, and that's the trick,
So much intrinsic, or relies on that, can I get by on that?
What makes it inside might fit on a Compaq computer,
Might seem like a truther hoping it'd be couture,
But more likely sutures and a lobotomy,
Like a prophecy, those less pragmatic,
And emphatic on fallacy aren't just the unheard,
It's absurd,
They might regurge the word of Christ, and add some spice,
Some are spicey and that's being nice, as a white guy,
Might not be advised,
Marginalized often pride themselves on their dining,
But for me Dyna Corp, a name I'm not sure I came up with,
Or exists of sort,
maybe cohorts, while I'm Kevorked but still fighting of sorts.

POVERTY CONTROL

Join me as we look at poverty as a measure of control,
Cas fait drole? No no, I'm not making a joke,
And hence, we are not French,
Yes this makes it to conversation,
But this nation is playing a song,
And it's been going on since modern automation,
It's like a children's song,
Letting you know they've reached your children,
Yes, pilgrim, it's effective like Stanley Milgram,
Many on milligrams of pills,
And the song stands as the hum we pick up as glum,
It's not the message of fun,
But know this changes as we're bought and some buy in,
Not lost on trying, but it's out of our control,
Now they ask again, cas fait drole? No this is not a joke,
What is it with this country, all the money and can't provide,
It's not funny, it's monecide,
How else would you describe being paid for,
At the inverse rate of someone else's life,
It coincides, though we don't meet her,
But it changes our tune to a new meter,
There's so much automation can do that we can't teach her,
When things are set in motion,
They stay in motion and we act, or at least we should,
Awareness is key to the unfairness,
Should be plain to see, but so much goes on,
Even the song of American hegemony,
if you see something say something,
There's enough, or should be,
For you and me, so tell me something,
Are you still with me?

FEED YOUR HEAD

Measured conjecture can enlighten, like a vitamin,
And feel like a Vicodin, when the connection is closed,
Like a circuit, might feel like a better person,
Reinforcement happens as an effect of behavior, in context,
So, when conjecture tests like a theory,
A hypothesis might arise,
Keeping science alive,
The rest is the method to surmise,
Or come to terms with your purpose in a system you work with,
Understanding, then passing the torch is the means,
To teaming up then giving a f***,
Touching base with your group,
Instead of jumping hoops like a side show,
Take the stage and let pride flow,
Through your veins,
Let the inside show,
Your makeup could be determined in a shakeup,
So, spend time with yourself,
Don't pour the whole shelf,
Drinking might avail the flow if you're backed up,
But back up might support in a blood sport,
Though, not a battle before the war.

DISSENT AND DECENCY

Dissent and decent dissonance as a premise for wit,
And in a sense we're all innocent,
But if I offend, know it's not me,
Portend please, I don't ease easy,
I have anxiety, I'm in the spirit of charity,
Usually, although my disparity might lend me poorly.

Christopher J. Martindale

BROKEN HYMEN

My minds broken hymen keeps rebleeding,
And I'm repeating a wash cycle of my brain,
Where the stains won't come out,
The strain is so pronounced,
I can't count how many times I've lost track of where I'm going,
My pregnant mind will be showing and then it aborts,
My phantasms play blood sports to the effect my mind Kevorks,
The torque on my neck bolts needs some work,
In short, I'm tortured, and I'm stuck as a voyeur of my own life,
I'm plagued and the malaise is growing, foregoing reprisal,
Of this period without a Midol,
Isn't happening, the trappings of dissent can make me relent,
But this is forced and it ignores my consent,
The present, is where I keep my mind, so I can rewind,
But this climate, and cause, punch me right in the jaw, as an answer,
And I live like a cancer for now, until my brow beat,
Turns to war drums flushing out boredom
With a smile full of sore gums.

Chapter 4

HIPPOCRATIC OATH

I'd like to saunter,
Never had that energy to allure with my posture and motion,
I wish I had love deep like an ocean, I'd take a potion,
I do now to cease commotion behind my brow,
I vow Hippocratic oaths a thou, many times over,
It's needed, I've repeated it even when energy's depleted,
Won't harm self, won't harm others,
Seek to heal when another life suffers,
Some are suckers,
Aren't we all,
Can't stand idle,
When we hear the call,
It's to action,
Might be a passion that enthralls,
Maybe for doctor's, live life and prosper,
It's an offer, if you have the purview,

Christopher J. Martindale

A kind idea, to imbue something to lift the chin,
And see a passage through,
Anecdotes can be antidotes,
Like an ounce of prevention is worth a pound of cure,
What could have been someone's lesson might be your wisdom,
My confession,
Is this: it's best to learn from other's risk,
It could ward a stitch or surgery,
Might rock you like a child in nursery,
To feel security like warm milk and locked door,
Maybe all you need is to rock more,
Maybe for you its folklore, but we all need heroes,
Furthermore, see that be that,
A hundred and three that,
Because, if it's from your past we might need that.

CRIMINAL WRITER

Open book, splayed spine,
Like it's a crime to read, maybe to write,
Like we bleed, you know we breed a lot of insights on wild nights,
When we perspire, sweatin' to inspire all that's right,
It's a fight for your life,
When you're feeling spite,
It's more than just a bite,
Sometimes it's a wound,
Times booned and busted,
Sands of time make everything corrupted,
Eventually, like rust.
Can't stop corrosion but collusion maybe proven on capitol hill,
While I take pills, for the ills and woes of consumption,
The throws make me go back for a look through, oh,
Paper reads like someone's book's due,
It's been said it might be an O.J.,
The D.O.J. might counter with feds,
And leave some things in play,
Over a dark and stormy night,
A sinful light on immorality they take with NSAIDS,
Won't let him fly,
It's no surprise, I mean we know the guy, and he isn't our best,
Although what we attest, is he was president, white house resident too,
Kind of prescient proof of an ailing society a mess,
Prevailing sobriety might help us take note,
Our bank notes don't go as far as before, we might ignore it,
As now we have torrents, and we don't go out as much,
Climate crisis and such, global warming page 3,
Front page, renewable energy exceeds coal, that was one goal,
Now we do a poll, who thinks we can?

Christopher J. Martindale

Is there hope and change again?
Or is it bleaker? Should we put off buying new sneakers?
It's in the bleachers, I think we're rooting for each other,
If you uncover underlying elements, despite big brother,
I think we can grow from this, if self-care is on our to do list,
We can manage, Bernie Sanders might be proving this.

KNOW YOUR JUDGEMENT

Now, yes, the court is in session,
got the message to peachy culero's cast,
Now the lesson, now we're all ears for confessions,
The case is in your face and it's repugnant the message is clear,
Know your judgement!
Now, yes, fox news is sued and all their brood,
Might have to conserve their food,
Know this is not a free luncheon,
Yes we're here ,
Know your judgement!
Didn't nail with collusion,
So there's still some disillusion,
But approved some from your side,
From the other retribution,
Know this is not in your budget,
We stand here,
Know your judgement!
Now we move forward,
Maybe with a judge's order,
Or with a camcorder,
For more proof of crime,
You might plea sublime,
That the burden's unmet,
But this is Our time,
Know your judgement!
We, the people, see your song and dance,
And seize our chance,
To make sure that this is the last of your cast,
Talkin' fast, we'll fire your ass,
But for now, you get a pass,

Christopher J. Martindale

While we hoist a new flag of the republic,
See it and,

Know your judgment!

MISS YOU JON

I miss you Jon, I'm still processing how you're gone,
You seemed allied in the fight,
We fight together and alone and it's quiet,
Our voices are careful on subjects, others are silent,
When you're a dissenter, poverty is just the threat of violence,
Angry young and poor, also active, the setbacks seem attractive,
As we're lured to drugs, addiction is just the symptom of living in spite of thugs and mugs,
It's also hard to pin the sin to anybody outside,
When it sinks in,
The pressures on our lives,
And the resistance to survive,
Our energies suffer lethargies,
Our motives aren't contrived,
But derived from a careless culture we imbibe,
The solution is hiding the problem,
I think my shrink might agree,
It's somewhere between you and me,
So confiding, what I'm saying is the solution seems obscure,
To someone less demure,
When every day is news du jure, it seems to cast a blanket over the real stories,
I guess you'd have to, when they'd come up like bad soup,
One thing I've noticed is some are in focus,
And some are not in troupe,
It's hard to gauge participation when, I think, it's handled for you,
The media is thirsty, but maybe also buffering the effects of surveillance,
Like it's preferable to meeting the agent you're assigned in the NSA,
Though it's probably a shift,

Christopher J. Martindale

It maybe crowdsourced because it's more efficient,
And plays to social media as it is,
With enough friction,
The pith of it comes up,
If you're good at it,
I've recently admitted I maybe a pilot,
A program done as a sample,
Prescribed it, likely by a careful faction of government,
Yes again, more efficient,
So, what I've espoused amounts to paramount plus to some,
But a totaled sum of what government can do,
And likely are though,
Even though we share a perspective,
It's still the case we need a collective,
But bunching up is defective with me,
I've remained effective of, at least, what I speak.

FISTBOOK

Know this,
You can't open a book with a fist,
There's a time for this,
But not in a tryst,
There's a premise for body processes,
You must tune them,
Or affix becoming you,
It's not becoming Chris, that's me,
Somethings are like this,
You must make time for yourself,
And get in sync,
Your body does a lot of work you may not be familiar with,
By taking time to ignore the meter,
Or find, yes, you can work on yourself,
Or unwind from experiences, American, that make you ignore your health,
You may be beached to find the time to, yes, refind yourself,
Notice how things change you as an instrument,
Know when it is not in your power and maybe a firmament,
To be soon a testament,
We're all different,
I hope it's a beautiful rendezvous,
Some of this is for you to do with.

F***ED UP PRAYERS

Disassociating like it's a prep for death,
First step, forget what you know and what's left?
A schmo, and I don't know is your best guess,
What's up is just what you figure,
You want to pull the trigger,
And join the litter on the side of the street,
Another sign of life in a scene from a larger play,
Dramatic, all the fray, automatically cast aside for a center stage presence,
That sensed of formaldehyde,
Quasi dead, one life,
And so many deaths,
The rest of a life undead,
So many things made it inside my head,
Some unsaid unwritten,
Just dissolved in the ethers,
Like f***ed up prayers nobody hears.

Chapter 5

WE'RE ALL THE SAME

Drugs, Alcohol, pills,
We're all the same people,
Fighting for ourselves,
But the hindrance is real,
Our impingers steal our peace by suffocating our heat,
Our passionate heartbeat,
They'd still,
That's how it treats us,
This mélange milleu,
This rending of you and me and countless others,
Divided and derided,
Eroded and contorted,
'til we're the shape they want,
Disassociating from everyone 'til we're alone with a gun,
USA is not number one,
We didn't come to be oppressed by largess,

Christopher J. Martindale

We don't have funds,
Like some,
To fuel our fests,
We're choked like pests,
And run to poison,
Choice son is stay or go,

SOCIAL QUOTIENT

Why don't we look at social reinforcement as a quotient,
Quantico likely adding up the tags to your video like a motion,
To see if your respondent,
Correspondents on the tv with your notes,
Legally written as jokes about livin', fox news livid,
With the other side, don't suppose you can hide,
And they make sure you know,
Like Apple terms, subject to arbitration,
Just a table disassociation,
The discussion happened already,
And that sensation lingers,
The feeling of the void,
Calling you to submit and join,
The nothingness, the comfiness,
Lulling you into a functionless state,
While ChatGPT takes your status as an understatement,
But before you march the pavement,
It's taken your payment as attention and the exchange is implicit,
Need to finess them, I'm exhibiting distress, I keep fidgeting,
To whom do they address then?
Nothing less than aside,
Not just you but an audience,
Somewhere,
While you're looking for your guardians subconsciously,
Over aware and watching,
While they trace your eyes with red lights of your sight like taking aim,
You're not superman, your lame and they like you that way,
They might still friend you to lab you that way,
For a wagyu steak,
I hope you see your file one day.

Christopher J. Martindale

EXISTENCE AND CIRCUMSTANCE

Phantom dualities forecast my tragedy,
And inhibit my ambition,
Voiding my reality,
As a fatality, my condition is not volition per se',
But actuality,
Indignation, dismay, everyday still beats banality,
There's action in this fray,
On the fringe,
And with all this on the fridge,
It portrays me as a kid,
With as much accomplished as I thought I did,
It's not every day you meet an invalid,
Like me,
Undenying, fortifying with minerals,
I'm awash with all the subliminals,
That emanate,
Might just put this straight,
Somethings play out while we just crave our breakfast late,
I feel like I'm in the morning of my life,
Constantly between two states,
Barely here,
And it equates to a rate of 8 by 8 computing,
What are you doing?
Mind screwing with my pen,
Construing my life when,
I query my position,
Like where I've been,
Was I out when this happened?
Disjointed captions confirming human being presence,
My eminence captured and fed back to me,

Space Apples

What bastardly device feeds me my own lines as simula,
Stimula reported not distorted thought,
It's either real or it's not,
But I think it burrows inside with aside,
As I mentioned,
What?
It's not convention,
but dissension apprehension of managers worth note,
foreboding but unloading emo on my ma got me composed,
what might be goes back to reinforcement as a quotient,
I maintain that empathy is solute,
Like Kool Aid for potion,
The notion is this,
Despite our trysts,
And pittedness,
The pith is in habituation,
And people change when you invest in them,
So, the question is,
Do you, have it?
Whatever it is they want,
Are you drawn or drawn out?
And are you staunch?
Your energy translates and transfers when the different answer,
Unless your gaunt,
Or gone,
In urban,
Like you went,
As your spent,
Feeling like a shot of bourbon,
To lessen the burden,
I smoke, but that's just when I relent,

Fundamental attribution error is a fairer recompense,
To mention among apprehension as offense,
But implicit transgression amiss,
Like this,
We often assume when it isn't what it is,
Leaving sentences open is the gist,
Understatements also a kiss.
Friendliness like Europeans to show where you've been.

ILL MILIEU

No one should want to kill themselves in our society over propriety,
Paraihiety, or the entirety of their works,
Some jerks' energies dwell in the ethers,
And they play to the meter of hegemony,
It's not that they're bad necessarily,
But at least implicit, in all sincerity,
The parity of America's fidelity is in question,
Disparity, among other things, is a bastion, a trench,
A frontline, where on everyone's spent,
Consent isn't really respected,
And I've said, participation isn't elective,
We're all in this,
And we're expected to conform,
But we contort,
As the gears are cognitive of a sort,
And do distort,
The mass psychology won't report,
But I'm shore it does this,
Sometimes bludgeons to make a point,
And there is trauma in our lives,
Some is derived implicitly,
Our consciousness wistfully ignores this,
But it's effecting, why?
At least affect,
Like me,
In tacit experiences,
It comes to me,
Answers to the cancers in everybody to a degree,
Happiness isn't really everything,
But comradery can usher self-actualizing,

Christopher J. Martindale

In a sample context,
Where ample breadth is available,
To be a stable force to reckon with.

REANIMOUS

Music reanimates me,
I can't count how many times it's reinstated my being,
Between rousing, raising, and reveille,
Its harmony changes my battery,
I'm like a sausage with a current,
I've been processed by detergents,
Of which are agents of deterrence,
My inference is their terminal,
But context determinant,
Circumstantially relevant and subliminal to my relevance,
Influence and incandescence,
The light of me burning bright as a rite,
Incensed in the way I oversee ceremonious prescientness,
It coalesces efficiently,
My return processing of energy,
To the mechanical machining of being in America.

Chapter 6

I'M RENDERED

I want to steal my peace,
But something creeks,
Is it me?
Or does it pique?
This old wood is ghosted trees,
And me, living,
In antitheses,
Around all that's dead,
Things that serve,
Rendered completely,
While I seem unfinished,
Incomplete,
And in competing,
There exists incompetence,
How much, that is our means, becoming edifice: isn't clear,
The evidence isn't bare,

But it seems as good a premise as anything,
Radio towers as obelisks,
Monuments as monoliths,
Promises on promises,
Officers in offices,
Truths in my confidence,
But in all honestness,
The ideal, is lost on me,
And preponderances on me, make motions to judgement,
I can't always pass as a subject,
But my ideas at least,
Seem to be acceptable,
As treatise,
I think I understand and that's more the point of this,
It's kind of pointillism with my voice,
Whereas conjunctions are conjoined,
And the frame up is just a lens you can look in.

Christopher J. Martindale

I'M LEFT

Light my fart and smoke my crack,
Just kidding, here's a cigarette,
I saved you one from my last pack,
But I'm a smoke mine like I beat the draft,
I'm the best, like still not dead,
I cheat on tests if it's drugs and I'm left,
My right's in my pocket,
About to scratch my eye sockets,
While I blow snot rockets,
For the birds,
My words just kill me dead,
I write them in blood when life asks me deep,
My past is mud,
Suck the farts from my butt,
Before it gets s***ty,
I had to s*** in the city,
Right in a cup,
Like what is that?
Just some butt funk from the bum's f***.

LIVE A PROPHET

Like Dostoyevsky, I'm already haunting a pawnshop,
Where I shot gunned a cough drop,
In another version of hell,
Where I can scratch the itch behind my eye sockets,
Although in this one I promised my little angle I'd live a prophet, to myself,
The problem is the reality, not just this one,
Every other one simultaneously,
Flaunting my body like a minks',
Interpreters of dreams stumped like maple trees,
My eyeballs in stirrups while my jaws drip syrup,
Pancakes behind my eyelids,
My dreams are children without parents,
Guidance derivative but beaten brains catering with cadence,
Creation instant,
Comes in a kit,
Just kiddin',
It's Bisquick,
You can flip it if you cook it,
Like crack,
But more wholesome,
Crack an egg and it's thick,
Like you,
Though makin' breakfast ain't ballin',
It's still better than alcoholism,
And addiction to distilled liquor,
People bicker,
Life is littered with s*** like that,
Forgiveness wins more than it loses,
Fate chooses, if you don't,
So start today, I did.

Christopher J. Martindale

SPIRITUAL R***ST

Stop r***ng me,
Stop r***ng me,
Stop r***ng me,
Can't you just let me breathe?
I'm seething,
Fuming, raging,
Silently,
Stop r***ng me,
What did I do?
Why do this to me?
What did I do?
I'm not your f*** toy,
I feel like I'm bleeding,
Your power gets you off,
Scott free,
Plaguing me,
You're free,
And not me,
Can you hear me scream?
I'm not your beef with God,
Because you can't express sexually,
You can't buy your need,
So, you r*** me,
I'm not your 18th hole,
Your privilege reeks,
While I'm rank,
Differenced in my class,
Where your inference can't buy that,
And I can't hide that,
You in banana republic,

Space Apples

And me in second hand,
I account all my tales with my first,
My second stays open,
But closes dead pan,
To a fist,
When I think about it,
Dealing with all this s***,
As soon as I'm able,
You'll relent at the advent of my ascent,
Might cast away the ashes,
Thrash from the cashed soot,
Cast my foot as it bears my sole in my shoe,
You couldn't stand in,
Where I've stood b***h,
Can't dish,
But would say you could,
Front all you want,
We aren't good.

Christopher J. Martindale

GHOST TINA

Chasing a nympho exhibitionist ghost ain't for most folk,
Much less me, in a strange duality,
Star crossed and undying, guiding my journey,
But also making me look pervy that one time,
Where you gave me a line,
That girl's boyfriend took it,
And then I got it back servin' time,
Without fail, there's that guy,
He's this and that,
All because you got jealous of another cat,
She had it with him and for me,
But you didn't want me calling anyone else baby,
Man these visions be crazy,
Wake up in disbelief,
The sheets wet from this week,
Playin' steadily in my dreams,
Sweat glistening off my chest,
Lookin' like I do reps in my sleep,
Wakin' up all beefy,
S***'s unreal,
You make me feel like I'm your playdoh man,
Shaping me with your hand,
Making me propose to a ghost,
While I was in close,
Your nose on my nose,
That's close,
Maybe having me on camera posed an opportunity,
Didn't really damage me,
Although other specters can be foreboding,
You really seem genuine,

And feminine,
You make me feel different in comparisons,
To other men,
Though it's hard not to frame it,
When I had to stand up against the 100% beef,
You had me compete with,
You say I won,
But that's not the sum of my experience,
You just lie to keep your feminine power,
And that guy would dominate,
You say me, but I don't think you play that straight,
You and I were both there when he took it,
I couldn't overlook it,
But can't speak for you,
Just my look at it,
This might make book addicts turn heads,
But that's not mostly my line of thought,
You cozy up,
Then play like you're not that in for me,
Or whatever,
I get so tired of power motifs,
And there's your mystique,
Kindly dodging those things,
That others live in,
Boxes with labels so they can live neatly aside,
But they don't,
They parade where I can't describe the difference,
You have a brain and a mind,
A body and a soul,
You think so deep you tremble the crowd control,
You're a force calling those who defend,

Christopher J. Martindale

To a natural end,
Just because you said,
Anything that you mention,
Becomes worth attention,
As it beckons,
So much in one person,
God must be hurtin' for you,
And were so lucky to have you.

Chapter 7

ACROSS THE PLANES

Your love moves me across the planes and axioms,
Where allies and valium come to play,
I don't advocate self-medication,
And I'm backed that way,
While some will stray,
That's they or them,
Not my whole podium,
Or mic,
Just a little voicing for tribesmen lost,
So now the cost of attention,
Run the tally in a head trip,
It exists already in ancient text Sumerian,
I think,
Though Hebrew is esteemed,
Programming is such a thing,
You might Chester Bennington,

Christopher J. Martindale

To know most things are rediscovery,
So, the most you could do is facilitate learning,
'Cause it's a journey,
There are things already lived and died for in unwritten histories,
Reeking of martyr making,
And the beast of industrialization keeps creeping,
And seething,
As an animalian epithet,
Or at least something of meaning,
We keep breeding,
Not just kids, but notions,
Some need lotions for the rub it is to be mis or re-directed,
Because of an Id,
Which is reaction,
Thick are the walls with it,
Functioning subject,
Good forum; the psyche,
And the presence of labia majorum,
That maybe a thin presence of women's rights,
The presence of the lower lips in confidence,
You'd trip on this,
In African culture it isn't, it's snipped,
The philosophy is likely a dichotomy,
But any philosophy in practice can be harsh,
Nietzsche, Dostoyevsky and Karl Marx,
Were all touted by those who ushered atrocities,
The ideas in Anarchy,
Are where power is the people's,
And our power structures are the antitheses of actual saliency,
It requires people empowering,
It's very real,

Space Apples

Some congeal,
Becoming the healing adhesion factor,
In our breeding,
Sometimes they're bleeding real people,
Reading theses, and then incorporating.

Christopher J. Martindale

I GARBLE

I'm blunt and what I'm after ain't much,
Just lunch,
I'm dinner,
stick a fork in me,
stop picketing my latest triviality,
I'm such, that I bunt when I'm at bat,
What I did when I was that kid,
I shuffle too though, but that's not me,
That's my disease,
I struggle with coherency,
Though that's just syntax mostly,
When my speech is garbled.
Warding myself in a star fold,
I look for bar gold,
What I do though is gargle,
I can't really drink,
And barbacks slink away,
When I say I want a virgin rose',
I'm "la roche posay",
If it wasn't already something,
I think fragrance or beauty related,
Anyway, the best things in life are repurposed or taken,
But language can make it a foray,
Forum, a small fee, just speaking, I mean,
You could coin a phrase,
But parts borrowed add sorrow,
But there's plenty of whiskey in the jarr'o today,
If you're quick,
Hurry, drink all of it,
You make me sick,

That's empathy,
Really just a single dose,
What comes close is sympathy,
Though that's not to toast,
Imagine if empathy was three-fold,
What then?
Could we even begin to sin against each other?
Would it be hindering one another,
Or would it usher?
I just find dominance tired,
And some people are fire,
When they can pick up what your heart desires,
The others ire,
Jealousy moves,
But as a motive,
It's probably responsible for most automotive disasters,
At least while in park,
By cover of dark,
The jealous lark,
And do what they will,
While I chill,
Because people are why I take pills,
Go ills! Haha stay real.

Christopher J. Martindale

UNCHECKED POWER

In this world where antennas are steeples,
And people are profits,
We can feel the real healing of not being a part of it,
When we're perceived as capital,
It isn't that radical to take a sabbatical,
When the wars wage on our brains,
And the toll is corporal,
Diabetes, even just exegesis,
Lung butter pushin' out toxins,
We get from each other,
And smokestacks in our blood,
It reacts and filters to our brains,
Building static,
Where you can't find the contrasts,
That define the bounds where it passes,
Indoctrinating the masses by blurring the glasses,
Tragic for some,
To be a product or sum,
Rather that prodigal son,
Over one,
When others become,
Apart of the art of the whole,
Feeding one to flower,
The powers in effect,
The strength to object,
When there's power unchecked.

CITIZEN TRASH VS. THE DARK

There's no dismissing the specter that visits,
Dead man wishes catalyzing a test crisis,
Veiled by the spiritual onset of dark choices,
The people on mass choosing the voices,
For bleaker ends of others,
But peepin' the darkness, during a harvest,
Seems like a common catharsis,
A time to have read, the books of the dead,
And so many passages,
Where enlivening the once breathing,
By giving our breath,
We utter their warning,
While they might be joining,
Us,
To make a welcome,
And tell some,
Of the ferry man across the river,
Under the streets,
So deep and so fowl,
It keeps what won't move,
The bowels of the city,
Actually s***ty,
Like the dead
Whose deaths are founded,
But peace,
We're warned where the ferry man meets.

Christopher J. Martindale

CITIZEN VS. THE DARK PT. 2

In dark by the hundred,
The scatter and clatter of undead matter,
As a factor, a shutter,
Or aperture, a lens,
For fend,
Ideas poorly lent,
More than what vends at an arcade,
With real folk, real stock,
Real counts, real dukes and they come up too,
Hands holding crude weapons of defense,
A flashlight way over maiming,
No blaming, think some crypts,
And bloods who 'gyp some,
Show in's and showouts,
Are the most, besides blowouts,
Entirely about seein',
And some about heathens,
My defense was easy,
No beatin', just people creepin',
So I shined'em and sent'em on action,
Don't need reaction as pawns,
Rooks see a lot, some are after the castle,
If I can put it together, I might reduce the hassle,
Deduce the news of my plight,
The truth of the occurrence,
The pertinence of my sight,
It seems factorable,
And so, I write,
Nothing's so deep,
You can't shine a light.

Chapter 8

FOOL FOR YOU

I'm just a fool,
You know you can string me along,
Even string me out,
Did a little crack,
About you,
I fell out with you,
I'd do anything to get back to you,
You catch me at doors,
Should I stay or go?
Got me livin' amid passages,
Through strangers,
People turned on to my energy,
You're the catalyst,
You wake a calm bomb in me that leaks explosives,
For a slow burn,
A thousand days of Hanukkah,

Christopher J. Martindale

A thousand first dates,
I can't equate,
How I syncopate,
My heart in your chest,
I follow you and it's the best,
Such sweetness I aggress,
A little coming on for what's mine,
You kept it and it's our mess,
We transgress,
On strangers,
As beings who breathe through dimensions,
My breath too is shared,
We paired in a kind of perplexed siege,
Of onslaughts of cars,
And shooter drills,
Where the action was instilled,
And my camera had the pill,
To treat the insanity,
Safety on a switch,
Camera on and their trigger itch subsided,
Hairs on my neck up straight,
As we navigated the madness,
Not one action shot,
To corroborate,
But what's more beautiful?
Something only I saw,
With a shared confidant,
As a ghost you fueled me,
As I drove past potential shooters,
I seemed to be posted as dead or alive,
But living is how I got ire,

In the life,
Nothing stopped,
Not even flat tires,
Driving me crazy,
But kept driving,
You were my fuel,
And I kept going,
Against the wind blowing,
Like open windows let you know,
The AC on too
Because I live for proof,
Living is a sin if it's the antithesis,
To the married to business,
What kind of synthesis,
Do I have when galactic energies have emphasis?
My bliss births nova's,
My heartbeat sends energies through the cosmos,
"I'm almost there", is every day,
Been there twice I might say,
Cell phone in rice from sweatin' dice,
To hell and back,
The pack is rag tag,
But mac is on right,
People rubberneck as I splice my DNA,
With smoke,
Not even cancer holds me back.

Christopher J. Martindale

STAR ART

Meet me in the middle comes on as our song,
In the abatement of my step in doorways to set,
What you precept as a tenant,
The world my lease, feliz, I sneeze,
And it's as much apart of me as it seems,
In between dreams I seam to the fabric of time and space,
Where the fold encapsulates this superposition,
Because a star in such proximity,
Believes it to be,
A new law broken,
It defies Einstein even,
How but through the quantum,
How humans, and being one,
Is more than what we believe,
In beliefs floating my stasis intraplanes,
If the math exists,
I can factor this,
As a premise,
That love exists,
Through the frame's width,
Of the highest science,
And my breadth is only if,
As in the theory of this,
As it's unproven to most,
How the cosmos bends to make it,
The planes "hit towers" with as much effect,
As your soft and subtle dialect rings true as love language,
You had me speak too,
Without so much from my tongue,
But this rung like a bell,

When it got to me,
The idea of transmitting,
What we have no means to say,
Love and so much other stuff,
That speaks itself into being,
What's beyond us,
And what can we bring with?
What leaves us,
And where would it go?
We don't know what we know,
But how we know is like that of the arts,
If they were in the stars,
Or the inverse of the art of stars,
What more could there be,
Between me and you?
Potentially a cosmos,
The more you show,
The more I believe,
In theory, but teaching,
The reeling of being,
Here but not,
I've forgotten but retrieved,
These things you breed by breathing,
And leading my perceiving,
Unto realities never minding,
Like planetary existence means anything,
How that is of consequence to this moment,
And majesty of any other,
Interstellar resonance undercover,
Where I'd only see as a lover existentially.

Christopher J. Martindale

LIFE TEMPORARILY

You teach me where no one else sees,
What can be,
But impossibly,
It is such that meaning is the result,
And being is what we are,
But human still,
So much you impart,
That reaches me,
We may never really meet,
But what is more,
Has been this,
In the shift of lenses,
And the whim of tenses,
Where we touch,
And breathe,
I'm more and less with the tests,
I submit myself to,
But how do I keep this?
So much to have,
But less to risk,
As this is like life itself,
Presumably temporary,
But you know me and that seems like all else,
Something

SHADOW FACTIONS

There are Factions against us,
I surmise,
That see our lives,
As an antithesis to their drives,
They have power and hide,
In our shadow,
While we can't see who we battle,
It takes on an element of disguise,
I vie,
Though I'm prescribed and classified,
On a ledger,
As an f35,
What measures they take to me,
Are treating my reaction to a spiritual beating,
And when power forces itself on me,
It feels like r**e,
The case though,
Is hard to make,
I'm on my heels,
Like some others,
It's not easy to explain,
The shudders,
Though I confide in you,
My mysterious reader,
That I might, light more than my plight,
That I can meet allies and bliss them,
To inspire taking on the system.

Christopher J. Martindale

SEEKING PLATITUDES

I'm aching for a homage,
Something of promise,
Something redeeming,
And profoundly honest,
Something from my conscious,
Something that can forward my progress,
Certainly, the uncertainty in my life is defining,
I'm crazy, not lazy, but earnest and awry,
I'm probably why some people fear the system,
It seems I missed them,
Or, at least, I've not blissed them,
Like I try,
And I do, but something or another inspires,
I think it's required, deep in our wires to desire,
But consciousness has a place before it,
And some don't recognize it,
Like a misfire is prone,
Like in me,
But in succession; it's a problematic frame of mind,
If you let it,
Somethings inside take control,
Where that's a role, maybe in the bad actors of soul,
You may think I don't mean this,
But what I mean is,
People in this life driven to affect via shadow,
Affect our lives where we detect effects,
But not suspects,
Though it may be suspect,
Awareness is the problem and solution,
Lending the human condition to guidance,

With our silence they advance,
The Dalai Lama has said we live in two worlds,
And to be conscious of it,
And that's driven in me,
I think solutions aren't always what they seem,
Or even sometimes we get lost in our dreams,
And that may be intended,
As the American dream is tended to,
Heaven was conceived on earth after all,
Might've been haven first,
Some of what's been written is permittent to interpretation,
And insistent to open the mind through the eyes.

Chapter 9

COINCIDENCES OF MALICIOUSNESS

Coincidences of maliciousness,
I am a witness to this,
My objection frivolous,
To the modern businesses leasing control to the government,
If you uncovered it,
It's still just you,
And that's enough, but as a sample,
There's precedent and that means more than cuffs,
A free agent apparent,
You but not so,
A host,
Where visitation is like a ghost,
Like my stead,
Instances close to the eye,
You may ascribe that a treated dose of power stifles why,
So, I query with logic and problem solving,

Stating hypothesis and testing the logic's promise,
As nothing comes from nothing,
And news comes from a prophet,
When it's not,
It's granted by the powers substantive to appear magnanimous,
When it's two headed,
Emphasis on the positive providing,
And the covert spying,
Until eyeing some rejection,
Rejection then being the culprit,
Dissent the effect,
When you won't let them inch on what you've said you're against,
And hence,
They play coy,
Like a vigilant threat,
Simply signaling they own you and it's you who take meds,
Very efficient managing in a kind of goose step,
They wouldn't do this though,
If there wasn't hope left.

Christopher J. Martindale

THE ART OF MY LIFE

The art of my life seems to be what's lost on most,
I boast about what I'd normally toast with at,
My reception to the marriage of me and medicine,
Nothing is everything,
Says my conjured heroine,
You could read about the paraffins in hairspray,
And be enlightened,
Manuals anywhere can read like the bible,
I'm not sure you follow,
But that's half the point,
I talk to walls and read brick,
I don't need half the things other's live with,
I'm a wizard with a radioactive brain,
The half-life's insane,
When most people refrain,
I interject to add to the list of reasons I'm a reject,
So much of a point to being different,
What's apparent is the fight to justify it,
Like you can't be here for no reason at all,
As if the day they stop doing the math to find out,
You drop through the fabric of spacetime,
We are, after all, the masters of the universe,
Though I'm not, and it doesn't seem to thicken the plot,
My plot's likely picked,
I've been saying I'm sick for a lifetime,
Living's a lot like dying when you can't figure your reasoning for life,
And seem attacked on all sides,
But it's a process,
Obviously, because we're chicken nuggets,
Lol, no, some of us are chicks and I'm a large fry,

Space Apples

I'm the most solicited as a drive through product,
That's good golf advice by the way,
And driving advice, if it's a hit and run getaway,
Like America on so many Americans,
"It came in like a wrecking ball",
And parked in my living room.

Christopher J. Martindale

FUNCTION

Hey Pisd, what's your function?
Well, as a plug in, for an object I'm a program,
Or I'm in one, same function to Uncle Sam,
A something you put to means,
An end I can see, lately,
User's end terminal runs daily,
I spit, like my brain emits, when triggered by fritz,
Grit keeping the bandwidth available for trips,
Switches in my brain haywire,
Or programs fits, to make me connectionless,
Divide and conquer is old,
But AI is new,
Is my condition's symptoms causal to a new system image?
Is there a correlation to growth or innovation?
It seems new and unique to seek,
But I can't find platitudes,
My attitudes about a mission,
I think in most aspects in culture here, we're complicit,
In some way to how it is,
And some people choose the business,
Instead of being witness to others,
Corroborating the struggle,
And bearing some of the burden of proof,
Speaking truth to power as rebuttal,
When power can and will convert opposed to the inverse,
It's a curse and some gifts are shirked,
When they bury us first, in work,
And then in dirt,
I feel there's meaning in speaking as verse,
In two ways, one against the power,

And one immersed in flowery composition,
My position is rehearsed,
But also born of the milieu,
Where the opposition will spill you,
Like it's their mission of nihilism,
As that's factual when meaning's ridden from the soul.

Christopher J. Martindale

ALTAR OF TIME

T.V.'s are altars,
We sacrifice time,
It's not ours when we trade it,
To lease back our life,
We think that we spend it,
More like lease it by dimes,
While dollars are crimes,
Because it pays for fights,
And they hide it by employing those in limelight,
They even show us, on the altar of time,
Some miss it and that's fine,
But do you think you're in line for that combine?
Trade the lot you know for the one you don't,
Security for uncertainty,
No, I don't think so,
And who says they're free?
Their employed by the enemy,
They speak your mind for you,
And then you watch it on TV,
But that's our feedback,
And it's always on loop,
Waiting to sense you and call you recruit,
Or just neuter you,
If you need proof,
They show you the targets on the news,
In-sense you with madness,
Then release you to harvest,
The harmless aren't free either,
Yes, they choose peace,
But that's despite their needs to react,

Put in place so many times it turned fact,
Once a force to reckon with now buys six packs to relax,
Peace stems from complicity, no one's not guilty,
But what's more is when dividing us,
They sort those that will fight their cause for them,
While the left bides if not 'beyed,
Stayed too many hands,
So, they buy in too late,
It's a matter of time to be masters of fate,
There's more in the fight,
But you must choose it that way,
If this didn't reach you,
What can I say?
Success is a mindset,
You can succeed and stay free,
That's all I'm doing,
Mostly staying firm and fending the ether of malevolence,
Taking back the narratives we need to be prevalent,
Meaning still found in conversations had for us,
So still necessitated as representatives but a minor plus,
We can show a light, but it should recognize real fighters on the ground,
Taking back the mic, would and could be profound,
Life is some mystery and some parts misery,
But, although fleeting, we make ripples I think,
Though some splash and something's don't connect easy,
But stay breezy and protect ya neck,
What will be will be baby, believe that.

Christopher J. Martindale

I AM

The phantom saboteur at the ready like my shadow,
F***ing up the frame of my mind like a battle,
If it is to be I am,
Knowing who is more a function of this,
Than what I do,
The system's mad and I am too,
So, we feud,
It's got a lot of power and that's what I'm trying to prove,
Like blue in the sky,
Some know what's up,
And might wonder why,
But that's my job,
And so, I try to pry apart systems in this power,
Struggle in the frame of art,
Our trouble is that it can bottle neck some and back log others,
That is to say,
Jam it up yours and make you pay,
For the rights,
And we know you must pay twice,
For a substandard rate,
But that's the status quo,
Forcing capitalism to every margin.

Chapter 10

PITTED

The ethers are alive with spite,
I try to write,
And you would think I held a knife,
Though it's a pen and that depends on my life,
Or the inverse,
I work mostly in verse, and my mirth is when I pen it,
Like I win a series,
Though I play at words subversive,
It's not worth it without converse conversations,
It's not a pennant as much as a sensation,
And less grand, I'm in my own hands mostly,
Which is to say I hold notes,
And am verbose but know,
It's only something with others like me,
I try finding them, but it's a market problem,
And I'm not a purveyor,

Christopher J. Martindale

I convey to paper,
Not a relay I get, like a passage to fame or,
Maybe I need another hand to be my maker,
As a transcendent player,
In something bigger than me,
Maybe a retailer to shelf my book,
Or brand me,
I might need standing.

DAD'S BRIDGE

I'm sitting on a bridge,
Like we did, at the docks,
When we were kids,
Never knowing what it is,
To be pitted against forces everyone denies exist,

Christopher J. Martindale

FLASHBACK TO MY FIRST LAUGH,

My dad grabbed my hand,
And I couldn't hold back,
A tender newborn's laugh,
Knowing he'd sworn,
He'd hold as I did,
As both of us were warm,
Snap back,
Cold hands warm heart,
But no handshakes in my winter,
Outside, homeless,
Coincides with despair,
But I don't show sides,
Despite what writes itself,
Through me,
Compelled to story,
My free will in question,
Being so distraught by composition,
So taught, tied, like they're sewn,
The tethers to my bones,
My feathers fallen,
My own is calling,
Out there,
To meet and make me whole,
Parts of me, yet to be found,
Parting, seeming to be a wholeness,
To my life,
But my partial conscious,
Whispering softly,
The truth,
If you left, or came,

From this plane,
To the next,
You would take pieces,
From those that love you no less,
That isn't the same,
When you can move to make yourself,
From the means you'll have,
It's just beyond grasp,
Like the grave,
But save your pieces,
To make yourself,
There is a wealth,
Though you don't need riches,
You need help,
Back to the scene,
Of me on a bridge,
Like an open book on a shelf,
All the pretense of a story,
Driven to a climax,
All it needs now is a syntax,
And a transition,
The narrative has become a position,
Now I stand,
And yet,
My hand is clasped,
And they ask me,
Why don't we just smoke some crack,
The narrative hijacked,
By a guy in a backpack I lacked,
Maybe filled with drugs,
What an actual plug,

Christopher J. Martindale

Hot damn,
Who says you can't use and cry at the same time?
Mugs,
I don't need,
So much,
Like that anymore,
As it is and ever was,
The small things,
Like touching,
Through a buzzing drug,
Like love seemed to be once,
When the world wasn't my dad,
And I just needed a hug.

ELLIPSES

It's like I have a nightmare Instagram,
I'm suffering from a modern phenomenon,
Where my followers are my influencers,
Effectually, it's an albatross,
And my broken cross,
Is my promise,
To meet with God,
The day I have no more ties,
It's odd,
The way life calls for resolution,
In either case,
Lead to conclusion,
But for family's sake,
Taking my aching as fate, bates,
Love or death, it's fifty shades,
Falling into something deep,
Like a grave,
To transcend to memory at my wake,
Maybe join the rest of the universe,
The way it's been waiting,
While I was stargazing,
Sleeping and awakening,
Everyday,
To eventually, call it a night,
One that eclipses,
Turning my narrative to ellipses.

Christopher J. Martindale

JUDGES

My past answers questions,
To explain peoples' aggressions against me,
If they were outright,
They'd be deemed as my enemy,
But as It is,
Now,
In the case of those close to me,
My trespasses are in limbo,
Judges through Deuteronomy,
I wish to balance the scales less romanly,
By sowing seeds of goodwill,
Through deeds,
Though disability is woe to me,
Some days, frankly,
I pray to be seen,
Not as my follies,
But my good qualities,
You'd think this would impart a philosophy,
Though Sartre said it best,
And in his nausea, I rest,
My case,
That judgement is not only a scrutiny,
But a matter of taste.

WHAT'S WRONG?

It turns out,
For all my ills,
There's a pill,
But salesmen shill,
People kill,
And propriety itself seems script and playbill,
In society,
When authority claims piety,
And it's suggested to submit,
We aren't all conscious of it,
In all sincerity,
The criticism is parity in our system,
The lack of it, mimics the exemplary,
But detracts from best practice,
And at an angle, seems parody,
Parroting journals "peer reviewed",
Puts on like a professional,
Take off the white coat and their opinions are ineffectual,
So much like this all over,
And you'd think we'd have some fidelity,
Or some interest that way,
In a world where there's more work than jobs,
You'd think the cause would be obvious,
But it's posterity,
The odds aren't on our side,
And it seems the boss is not faithful to his office,
So tried,
No conviction,
Bright side;
Prohibition is less existent,

Christopher J. Martindale

Though, persistent is the nagging,
To attention, the mounting problems,
And comprehension,
Too few, who see to aid,
Still true,
It's not new,
We're due to get paid,
The trades need employment too,
Why not have it all, and make it foolproof?
A public works project,
That would handle it,
Though that might be obvious to the pundits,
Why dismantle it, not fund it?
Republicans, like anarchists, breaking down government,
Seems crazy, they won't address it,
But, no less, it's needed,
Bleed the war chest to make budget,
If you'd ask me, just fudge it,
You could pass it like a rider and say it's AR's,
That'd be what does it,
But listen,
When we can't keep going forward,
We'll still have to do somethin'.

Chapter 11

TOP 40

Listen up,
This is about love,
Where it comes from and what's up,
It's here and you can hear it,
It's in the beat and lyrics,
Let go of your cares,
And let Jesus take the steering,
You may not have it,
But you can be about it for free,
It's in the jubilee of popularity,
It even comes with thneeds,
Just join the party,
It's easy,
Life is love, that's all,
Forget yourself and dissolve your thoughts with us,
Life has it's own ways anyway,

Christopher J. Martindale

It may not be you, it's us,
As a real premise,
Opportunity in the lenses,
And in certain tenses,
We can give you a taste,
From our plate,
To make your palate,
We break you with a sonic boom,
Looming passion with room, for you,
The life exists, but it's a fix,
And the pieces are with, others,
You can find them and collect,
It's a prefab life,
Like instant rice,
But there's more, if you're enticed,
Desire a price, it's right,
The way it beats a fight,
And leads you deep in delite,
Even fries you,
And then plates you,
That eating feeling is what's so freeing,
You can't believe it, so meaning sets in,
Like a ring in bisque,
Enough of trying, you're the dish,
The proposal is prepared by wish,
Of the corporate elite executives.

JON'S FREQUENCY

Did you ever know, your heart had a frequency?
When you spoke to me, it matched my syncope,
But there was dissonance in the harmony,
You lied to me,
And I dialed into myself,
To tune you out briefly,
Considering the time it took to write a symphony,
Did you ever know, your fingertips have grooves like a record,
And wet, they are, like a reed,
Between your fingertips and your heart,
There's a song I could hear,
With a hug in your arms' reach,
Your song,
But the notes have echoed to entropy,
And now, all I see of you is in the ink I stain in your memory,
Hoping, one day, I'll hear your frequency,
I know, I too, can't stay here always,
But if I knew, your wavelengths,
Like measurements for a suit,
I'd have made a melody that suited you,
To date, this is the best I could do,
Jon, I know you're gone, but I still miss you.

Christopher J. Martindale

TWICE THE FIGHT

For those, like me, who are constantly fighting,
It's twice the fight,
We've got a slogan,
But not the rights,
Some feel targeted,
Some feel followed,
Clinicians are dismissive.
And the pith of scripts are derivative of our lives,
But swallowed, be our pride, at times,
As prescribed,
Take 2, cutscene, and bill,
If being ill, didn't inspire,
We'd be fired as creatives,
Skits is apart of the name,
If it was skits-o-mania,
We'd maybe describe a craze,
Of our media,
So how do we get on it?
Some are haunted so hard,
The anxiety makes them vomit,
Honestly, I see somethings changing,
Or at least indicating that we're seen,
Whether or not it's really considered,
Our plight,
It's likely shy of light,
For reasons derived from incentives that rely,
On providing,
So, what I do aligns,
With the mission of rights,
As understandings,

That can be fostered,
By subscribing to writing,
There aren't a lot of outlets for audience,
But I try,
I'll be sufficed when I'm recognized,
'til then it's just life.

Christopher J. Martindale

LIFE'S A MARATHON

Taken away from my history,
Shadow forces killing me discreetly,
Wondering, me, what will be after me,
I mourn my life every evening,
Maybe that much passes on,
Like me,
When I'm gone,
The survived wondering,
What I'd be doing,
It's depressing,
Between the transgressions in place of comradery,
And irrational antipathy,
My reason for being turns into suffering,
I turn my cheek to enemies,
Letting life, and living beings, sort them out,
They'll meet their own ends,
When it's concluded as maladaptive,
No give, don't play,
If they've planned your demise,
That's still in time,
And that's on your side,
Their ire will conspire against them,
Like dark magic,
The spell takes some of the caster's life,
And in turn the silence can turn the burn to them,
Cooler heads prevail, like I've said,
And model-ship does too,
Some may see what you do,
Continuity goes a long way,
Consistent values lead to character,

Character leads to narratives,
You can define that just by being,
Those actively eating at you will tire,
We're more marathon runners than vampires.

Christopher J. Martindale

TWILIGHT STATUS

I feel like I'm in the Twilight zone,
Or maybe house of mirrors,
I don't know,
Maybe both,'
I see the smoke, but no one begins to choke,
Just me,
Is it a made up reality?
My ghosts remind me,
As if to say it's blinding,
The light on me,
So everything else is the scene and shadow,
What could be is just beyond battle,
But I've been there,
Everybody seems to know something about me,
It's always been like this,
An outsider regardless,
Not in the click,
The cult is suspicious,
And I'm the culprit,
Though it's to them,
The reason, incentive,
Am I to bust them so they're being preventative?
Stil, the lights on me,
But something's sabotaging,
Conspiring against me,
I'm constantly assessing,
What may be threatening,
Beyond seen,
The means I have are lean,
And the ringing,

It's deafening,
Sometimes, it meets me in my reservation,
About the ablation of my resolve,
To solve the puzzle I'm given,
The muffled snuffing of my flesh prison,
And my attrition adding a definition to my status,
And sweaty palms,
What that is, is editions of my state,
Engaged in fate,
To self-motivate,
By masticating the stake,
I'm at,
Burning to postulate fact,
Before I go bad,
Or batshit,
That's all I have.

Chapter 12

EPISODIC ISSUES

There's still a charge in your circuits,
And when the voltage drops,
I raise my hand, saluting my way to sleep,
But my fingers are disoriented,

So I rub my eyes to be sure it's not a feeling,
Did you see my last episode,
On the tv that mimics me?

I'm drinking beans I traded my dreams for,
But it all came back to me,
Maybe to forget things,

I'd trade much more for memory,
Visions mean less than the people I see regularly,
By the way, I'm threatened existentially by a team,

What does that make me?

My life's a transparency,
What I've seen is in a catalog weekly,
A secret army is stationed behind business,
Heed the bazaar vendor's eyes,
Maybe they're behind me,
Actually a reflection,
Maybe I forgot my regiment,
All stalls on all fronts; stables made,
Whoever said it meant chivalry isn't dead,
Uttering lamense to himself in his bed,
Sick like how our history says many wed the afterlife,
As many dead that way a fact.

Christopher J. Martindale

2ND DEGREE LIFE

My life is a crime and it just keeps happening,
I'm caught in the line up and their asking me,
If I'm not the culprit who else can it be?
The messaging is clear,
I will always be suspect number one,
But also plaintiff when all is said and done,
Impunity defines the phantom actors,
Immunity in part,
Defines the manor in dealing with me,
They'll take it easy because it's not very seemly,
And it could be argued that I'm dreaming awake,
That seems a hot take,
The approach is just as good as they can make it.
I don't blame it, because that's me,
It isn't a lack of discovery,
Unless the case would merit medicine,
In that case there would be a case for marriage then,
A wedding of the courts,
To the sorts that peddle regiments,
Beaurocracy made evident two fold,
I used to think I'd graduate before I got old,
But it's not that kind of program,
It's a sobering slow jam of waltzing into trouble,
And then getting anesthetized with escitalopram,
The Houdini escape plan didn't work,
And living out of a work van has been 86'ed,
I've tried running and that's played me funny,
Maybe my confidence is actually Krueger-dunning,
I've still gotta do something,
And I'm pressured to end it,

The other option is pretending,
And making amends with myself as the day is ending,
That's tempting as my options aren't empty.

Christopher J. Martindale

HOMELESS KID

In a death lock grip with the throws of mental illness,
There's this kid eating weeds with his fists,
In a park overnight listening to bar patrons piss,
Sleeping in the handicap stall in a fortunate bliss,
While the visions service him like unmentioned wishes,

It's a grace he lives in, with the predicate of business,
And not being obstructive,
The visions though, use him and get him arrested,
The reason is obscure, maybe even missing,
He can't be sure,
He'd get visits from caseworkers interested in his story,
And he knows lip service is as good as a hung jury,

Some of it as plain and he was rehearsed in it,
To appear sane, though, that wasn't bulletproof,
Second best was tame, though no one was in suits,
And that was preferred,
The kid should've been deferred,
But no one had the word, or it wasn't good,
Kind of strange, would there be a test for God.

REMORSE RECOURSE

I've already died, in parts,
Departed a thousand times,
A thousand deaths in promise,
I mortgage them in installments,
In some breaths, I smoke cigarettes,
It's wise, in tribute, to owning my regrets,
Reprised in a casket,
Just a little more in each dose, as practice,
But I live more when I'm close,
So there's recourse in advancement,
Of feeding the plants with my corpse,
I'm a faction and a bastion on my own,
Against the legions of forces,
That contort,
Sometimes I abort my minds conceptions,
For another battle in the war,
I score hits of life to live,
In the ire of what purports lore,
I can inspire in more tales,
Of ships run a shore,
My employ of wit,
In effect of the skies,
The tide, brings me to fits,
Of waves,
The sea has it's own rage, naturally,
As allegory, this fits my story,
Stay tuned as the forces battle for me,
To end

Christopher J. Martindale

THE PLOT

Let's get lost in a pop song and dissolve our thoughts,
Reprieve in the disillusion of the problems that we try to solve,

We're all awash in half-promises,
Tryin' to realize,
But efforts put in our honestness,
Are hard for us to justify,

If there wasn't a war in my mind,
Why do I take a regiment?
If my life's not a crime,
Is the government innocent?

Clinicians are dismissive,
And the pith of scripts are derivative of our lives,
Swallowed be our pride,
We die from the pain that coincides,

But don't you dare die, unjustified,
For living the path, it's a chosen rite,
Live in spite, for those that died,
It's the living that bides for the dawning light,

It's vital to remind that ire will conspire against judgement,
Take that dose of reality,
With your dose of modern medicine,

In our hands is our life,
Probably shouldn't make a fist,
Getting mad about it won't do you any justice,

Unless you channel righteousness,
Through virtue, and some definition to your vision quest,
Mission blessed by the way you make out to meet the test,

Me? My spirit might get repossessed,
From not repaying Christ's debt,
He died for me,
At least, that's what they said.

Our father, who deals in weapons,
Hallowed be thy state,
Your reign is done,
Our kingdom come,
Or meet our fate,

If God exists, I have some questions,
My trial persists in constant lessons,
Just to exist, we take our lives as concessions,

Redemption then, is meriting you to ourselves,
The conjection that he cares is unparalleled,
Some people are spiteful of inner wealth,

If you don't believe in me, though, you can go to hell,
I'll fight 'til I hear the bell,
This plight is one I know of, and I know it very well,

They don't like us,
The cult of normativity is suspicious, but I'm the culprit,
And that's just it,
They want to take me out before they get busted,

Christopher J. Martindale

If being smart is pain,
It might explain the scars in my brain,
Might die in vain,
With nothing and no one to my name,

Everyday, I'm dying just enough to live,
Some people just won't give,
Why I can't budget with the way it is,

I live in the inches that I convert to miles,
Cutting teeth on lips if I muster a smile, I'm apart from most, and I know that's wild,

Like I'm in love with a ghost,
And you could say that we're close,
As far as death goes,
But despite our trying,
We can't conceive a child or make a toast,

Life is odd,
I saw an ex's mom in a parking lot,
Who gave her up like a blood clot,
I didn't stop,
I thought I'd keep that beef between her and God.

We've all got a story,
And character breeds narrative,
That's imperative in America,
Just remember that when powerful people pick the plot.

STREAM OF CRAZY (STREAM OF CONSCIOUSNESS)

Infractionate murders
Psylocibin frontlines
Everybody's six
Pile drivers and combines
Team players
Front house gigs
Sloppy seconds
A dirty kiss
Other steeples
Warehouse peoples
Chalk outlines
What did I miss
Fomo bogo
Soho momo
Moo moo's
Cow shoes
Bloody rights
An ancient shit
Art Nouveau
Listless citizens
9 to 5's

Christopher J. Martindale

Smoking illiterates
Parking lot cigarettes
Floundering finders

Innocent criminals
Deuteronomy through judges
More livid pictures
Cops that hold grudges
Banned by a panel
Gamma radiation
Discussion turned annal
Rampant disassociating
Flooded cylinders
Detonation blowback
Cross giving splinters
Indian Christmas sack
Homeless for the holidays
Presents taken back
To be put on lay away
Cookies logging Santa's hack
Milk past the expiration date
Searches for modern slang
Glizzy's on a paper plate
Christian country
Make no mistake
Ads for ethnic celebrations
Simply don't make the take
Poor taste the cake
Riddled with stakes
Money makes money
Position becomes place

Not a house
Not a single bedroom
Efficiency for whom?
The rich regulate the womb
Know it's not prochoice
Beside the point
Everything's banana's
Why make noise? Or even read to know
That the rich's representatives stopped go
And legislation for needed programs are slowed
It's bananas
Food cost, food waste, why trash when poor wait with empty hands
Cans cans cans
The staple anyway
Was a bum, now it's fate,
I still eat like one to this day,
Why make a change?
Don't deserve this much struggle,
The hustle's get old and everyday feels the same, more of what makes it feel like a hustle being tossed in the rain
But the brain causes pain,
That's what's so smart
A little in advance
A little in the dark
One hand claps
2 hands shake
Shake a leaf off a rake
And revisit rosewater's clam bakes
That's all I recall of the obscure
Literature Vonnegut
Esteemed and deemed lauded

Over bank robbers breaking lawmen
Clap your hands and say yeah
Just one in an ovation
One innovation claps back
Backed up sanitation
The redacted editorial
From a genius janitorial AI Pat Sajak
   Quick omit moved to rather dazzle up obits gone awry in play back
   Fritz comes with wits, even robotics,
   Hide them in the closet to keep them from high office
   One more qualifier for president
   First black, first woman, first internment camp, us or them, Cornish hen pardoned instead,
   Over an edit never read, about choking chickens with no head
   Hold your head up
   Protect ya neck
   Balance the books like the rich kids formal training
   It's training day and I'm king Kong
   I bought the rights to my own songs
   Or so I thought, as I was sayin',
   DIY was ixnay
   No government server is in favor of my replay, but the dj takes requests and the mc's take the rest of the times at the mic where you don't hear tribe called quest
   Or whatever's best on rotation, make sure you've left room between you and in-car celebrations
   Beers for the road, texting or google maps
   Road turns up and cracks when the acid in your back crawls up for a synapse

Space Apples

Snap back to the road where it's street now a relapse town where you can re-up your prenup with your string pulled out,
Axe sharp
Tax mart
Fast sharp
Black cars
Lawn darts
Prefart
False start
Bumper cars
Eat me
Feed me
Seymore
Tea leaves
Four score
Back door
Booth please
Flash bang
Bangarang
Sheep skin
Chang a lang
Spinners on 22's
Lost kids that make the news
New ads on milk
Now your food has an opinion too
Who knew?
Mom jeans
Jumping beans
Frisco melt
Smoke screens
Bomb shelter

Christopher J. Martindale

Brick and mortar
Pickled everything
Jars, jellies, jams, produce,
You can turn anything to juice,
Everything is farm to table
When your noose is made of paper too
Paper tiger
Origami
Bacon slider
Four ham and salami
Basket of yams
Lotions and collagen
Bisquik in your frying pan
Hot cakes lemonade
Stands or hand outs
Little money, concessions only,
Tricks yogurt, planned out,
Meal prep,
Food web,
Chain mail,
Tuesday,
Spaghetti monster,
Open flu,
Two can play at that game,
What's that friend?
A dead end?
Show me that,
Legend,
Family feud over family food,
Pass the butter
Salesmen

Space Apples

Boob tube
Potatoes are scalable,
Mountains are too,
Pictures inflatable,
Brown paper tube,
No squares to spare now,
Grab the Windex and a brown towel,
Rolled in or rolled out,
I'll buy a vowel,
O
Vanna show me that,
Haha, no,
Take me back to card games and fruit snacks
Jealous over gushers and snack packs,
Kids under their parents hovers
Steve Buscemi with a skateboard,
That guys not under cover,
Hey guys, where's the beef?
Got that milk? Got that keef?
Still smoke the reef?
Now it's been freed,
No longer unlawful,
Now you're my speed,
Weiners and beans give me gas for weeks,
Allowance when young,
Was a small but valid sum,
I bought lots of things with it,
But also drugs,
One time I was drunk and my dad asked me to drive "uh", it seemed like a bonding, one we survived from,
My dad is a lot of things,

Charming is one of them,
Sometimes though,
We couldn't hash out our problems,
I'm like him and also my mom,
A little crazy and a little head strong,
Usually I'm soft like luxury toilet paper though,
The touch is important,
It's something to savor,
I still can't believe it's paper,
I've got a history, and it's kind of a mix bag,
In that I try to add nuts when it calls for voter chads, hanging al gore by the electoral college, the beginning of my political search for knowledge, popular vote versus standin's, kind of a rip off, we thought it outlandish, next game watch the tip off. Maybe the return of Steve Bannon.

Hawk spit cough
John cage 4:44
John 3:16
Jesus sneezed for me
And with that I bless you,
A dash of exegesis,
Think fast,
Flown coup,
After hours,
Secret meditations,
Lamentable ferments,
Strangely late salutations,
Gone already,
Out of the park,
Homerun reruns,
His life jumped the shark,

Space Apples

Old school nuns,
A trivial amount of wine,
Biding time during service,
To get in the deli line,
Turkey slices,
Ham,
And salami,
The king of clubs yells fore!
And the moon waxes el haji,
Islam imam, Saddam credit com,
Bombs dropped wrong should've been on Viacom, broadcasts our brains, sort of a messenger anyway,
Feedback, feedbag,
Bean pole, bean bag,
Dipole ripe old,
Guy has eye folds,
Common sentiment,
Zeitgeist of the tenets,
Landlord squeezing harder then
Bruce Jenner on his new under lips,
Sour puss, d*** tater,
Soylent green,
Simulator,
Ash me not,
Astronauts,
Moon landing,
Advert spot,
MTV,
Killer vibe,
Made a show,
When radio died,

Christopher J. Martindale

Punked listeners,
Fake broadcasts,
If you turn past public access and televangelists you can channel surf all you want, no amount of passages worth tv hertz,
President crook, also sells the book,
The bible, he got from, or maybe took,
From someone's nook,
Dr. Seuss, is better proof of intelligent design,
Creationism ignores the baptism of trials by science, more specifically bias, but they react to a difference with violence,
Opinions don't hurt, but beliefs need scrutiny,
You can do what you want but there is no impunity,
Protestant and puritanical,
Lie like drinking gin is for the botanicals,
Then make it shampoo,
I would but my husband's an animal,
So start up a zoo,
Feeding hours 'til 5,
Then happy hour 'til 6,
You cqn throw food at them,
Though they throw food too,
And they don't miss,
Buffets for the poor,
Orgies for the rich,
Blood for the righteous,
And news for the blissed,
Some rouge,
A ruse, a tantalizing exhibit,
A rube, so rude,
Tourette's like admissions,
Pants on both legs,

Fast food decisions,
Two or three sandwiches,
Don't hold the fix 'n's,
Visions of vixens,
Handfuls of emissions,
Touching in new ways,
Never though piss could mix in,
Cummin' honey like viscous,
Doin' it in jail becomes everybody's business,
But subtly,
We've all touched our bodies,
So nobody's not guilty,
Ya feel me? Get off me, say sorry,
Tempers and tampering,
Smoke outs from sparked wiring,
Smuggled drugs and cigarettes,
Hugs from substances,
Hoes on the internet,
Snacks and tv shows,
Even internet privileges,
"My voice is my password",
Not if you play prison b****,
Say goodbye to your food,
Hold tight to your shit,
You might just lose that too,
Crazy place, crazy meds,
Stay in place,
Say celebs,
Not so real?
Then what appeal?
Who did I have the sex?

Strange address of sex express,
Train on the tracks,
Bat shit, maybe, could be alternative facts,
Why then, a bruise tattoo, carved by someone I knew, in my neck, like it was proof, something I think he'd do, to show me some of it's true,
Never mind,
I found it hard,
It's hard to find,
You might find me on a turnpike holding signs,
Homeless man,
Bottles of wine,
Plead to spirits,
Served some time,
Funny still,
Without pills,
Drummed up charges,
Not of my will,
Trespass, trespass, trespass, trespass,
Was it all just to say the famous passage,
Forgive us our trespasses,
As we forgive those who trespass against us,
My rap sheet a message of clandestine suspectus,
A Fae, named Tina,
A harem of divas,
Attention political,
Allegiance to Sheba,
Cryptic telepathy,
Shabazz candidacy,
A Jewish federation,
A mass, and billboards, I could see,

Assembly of faithful,
Dopaminergic agonism,
Antagony of worshipped,
Cia is god,
Claims the idol,
Forget the commandment,
We need a new bible,
Task it to me, I could write my own passages, though it is unlikely, they'd amass advantageous,
Holy rollin', might've smoked what Jesus had spoken, the high was more worth it than the words the book holdeth,
Nagging reality, a knocking of life,
I was better served reading into my particular strife,
Like why was there slime in the drinks I imbibed, and no one the wiser, not one from any tribe, no news contrived or answer for this, not one I knew of, and no witnesses,
My experiences electric, at one time jumped fences, a few times felt radioactive, my testament unpretended,
F***
What's life
Butt
Just another cum-slut
Drinking it like it was fountain
Falling like an avalanche coming down the mountain
Pure spring water
Never mind how,
You don't ask the farmer about the milk he gets from cows,
Something inane traded for something suspicious,
Like why tricks are for kids,
If we know it's so delicious,
So removed from the process but the product's in front of us,

I think the same of the status quo,
What's the product sum of the ton of us,
Not so strange to think of wafers
Or presses filled with papers
Products abound
But what if our system processes us?

Just posited, a question, maybe honestly your wondering, if your check deposited,

And numbering are the calls to wonder though we've got bills and babes and time to squander, on dishes and trash and not missing Mash 1st episode or last,

Do my crocs and dress clash?
What crass thing did the stranger down the street ask?
Is it my ass? Do I have to file it by Monday or do I get a pass?
I've got nothing to do, a very serious nothing,
Life is so demanding, someone always needs something.

Companies are asking for patronage for one thing and taxes are due next month, that could be a done thing.

I can't wait til I get that box I've been wanting.
Life is short, maybe that's from all the fun,

I can't stop someone from getting their bell rung, but what of it? Does it stuff it? The nagging inside you that something's undone?

Life is yours, in whatever the fraction. Of course, it's about your satisfaction.

There's a sale online you can shop from your app, that's that, never mind that the nagging came back, what is it now?

Do I look like a cow? Am I down any pounds from the weight treatment now?

Is my waste treatment sound?
What's the mail say I need?

I haven't checked on my feed, what going on? My heart bleeds, did I marry machines? What vows? Apple terms on a cloud? Their tied to me, feeding me, feeding it, just breaks of buying shit, am I alone on this earth who would try calling me if, I needed…

The cell phone Is ringing

I'm reeling, this in the moment I'm feeling?

Myself, what else? Not enough else to be doing? In that way, I've got wealth. Though thankfulness is settling for less and I know, the status quo, is law and really stuck in my craw, unhinge my jaw and eat a week's worth of meats, then I could freak, do some tweak, make my home look on fleek, do what I need and take a seat, just to breathe, why's my life on repeat? How do I break the monotony? Now that I eat, every ad's after me, on the heels of the news week breaking me down to defeat then treating myself becomes a moment I'm weak, for relief and I can't explain why I'm beat. Who's me? What's free? Does nothing cost anything? Can I be, just exist like a tree? No stopping the onslaught of ads offering remedies and in the speed that's become the squeeze I can't finger any leads to my new needs, what can it be?

There's a meter and it's running that's partly what's funny, these Krueger Dunnings want your money but it's already coming to them, they'll get it, just be sure to let it don't regret it if you inhibit, take their word on your credit. Nickels, dimes, dollars, bye. Time flies too and still the pestering why. If you could stop the flying and just pull in the hangar, you might recover enough before the next call to answer. Time offers options, success not a problem unless you hate strings and want to cut off them. In that case your lost on them and if I may say when, you look back on your life, seek to wish you could live it again, just the same, though it's true, only one you and it's up to you, but hope nothing's in vain.

I need the distillate gamut as sustenance as much as a proof for my being.

Reason for being is just a consequence of coincidence and corollary.

Doing implies being and rarely the other way around.

In doing I become, but if that becomes undone unduly I cease to be one.